Also by Anna Rose:
THE SUMAIRE WEB:
Siofra
Fiach Fola
Droch Fola
Féasta Fola (short story)
Cosán Fola *(coming soon!)*

I0533228

This is a work of fiction. Similarities to real people, places, or events are entirely coincidental.

AYA'S DRAGON

First edition. December 30, 2017.

Copyright © 2017 Anna Rose.

ISBN: 978-1393739081

Written by Anna Rose.

To all of you out there who love dragons at least as much as I do!

A message from Anna Rose:

This story is separated into sections, rather than chapters, for the reader's convenience. I hope you find it to be a useful tool.

I have loved dragons since I was very young and knew that I would eventually end up writing about them. I am only sorry that I took so long to get around to it.

The first novel about dragons I read that left me wanting more was DRAGONFLIGHT, by the inestimable Anne McCaffrey. She wrote many more novels about the Dragonriders of Pern, and I eagerly devoured each one of them. I just could not help myself.

If you have not read them, I highly recommend that you do. Do not forget to read her Harper Hall of Pern trilogy, which is aimed at young people, but is still fine reading for the nominal adults out there.

Thank you to my wonderful, patient beta readers and editors, who have done a wonderful job to make sure I don't make a complete fool of myself with my writing.

NJ, Robin, Janet, and The Ape have been wonderful, and I want to extend special thanks to His Mooseness, who has always been especially wonderful to me in this regard.

In conclusion, I hope you all can forgive me taking this long to get this done, NJ. It should have been done a very long time ago. Now you can stop shaking your finger at me.

All my best to all of you.

Anna

1

The flight of dragons glided lazily overhead, the sun dancing across their shining hides, creating a living rainbow of prismatic color that reflected down onto the ground below. Enormous in comparison to the human riders they bore, the dragons made the scattered buildings below them look like a children's fragile playthings.

The nearest village was at least ten miles beyond the furthest buildings of the farm, over dauntingly rough and dangerous terrain. On horseback, a trip to the village could take an entire day, there and back once more. If one left first thing in the predawn morning, they would not return until long after sundown of the same day. It was not a journey to take lightly.

This particular plot of land, surrounded by rocky cliffs and uncounted acres of forest, was many miles from the nearest barony. It simply was not worth the time and effort of the closest local baron to add it to his holdings.

The entire farm was almost four acres in size. It featured a reasonably kept, whitewashed stone cottage, a barn made of mixed stones and heavily weathered lumber, a few patched and ragged animal pens, a small, fenced cemetery, and a little beyond that barn, a battered chicken coop that was now in the process of being cleaned. It was a young woman with long white-blonde hair pulled back into a loose bun at the nape of her neck and large, dark brown eyes that contained occasional flashes of copper and gold.

She was almost finished cleaning the coop, after a long, hot day of shoveling and scrubbing. It was thankless work as the hens, being only slightly above pigs in cleanliness, simply did not care how their home looked and smelled, unlike the humans who had to collect their freshly laid eggs on a daily basis.

The small flock of elderly hens that clucked at her, done for the day with hunting for juicy, protein-rich bugs outside, were disturbed by Aya's continued intrusion, as they wanted to settle back into their nests, and she had broken the relative peace of their comfortable, although stinking, wood and wire home. She wondered why she even bothered to do more than shovel out the collected manure, as it did not matter how much one scrubbed, the stink never went away. It truly seemed to be an exercise in futility.

After changing out the straw in the last two nesting boxes, it was a blessing to be able to step out of the cramped, humid coop, into the fresh, early evening air. Aya had to remind herself not to use her filthy hand to brush her hair, which had escaped its tether at the nape of her neck, out of her eyes.

As she gazed out into the waning day, she watched the rainbow-colored flight of dragons and their riders on their evening flyover, now traveling along the edge of the forest that lay about a quarter mile from where she stood. It took Aya a moment before she remembered to breathe again.

The dragons always astounded her, no matter how many times she might see them. Despite the creatures' great size, they seemed so very graceful as they made their way through the air. They dipped and soared, wingtip to wingtip, in a wondrous aerial ballet.

She did not remember ever having seen them on the ground, which she found surprising. You would think they would have to land sometime if only to rest the muscles that supported and moved their massive wings.

AYA'S DRAGON

As far as she could tell, they came in every conceivable color, and even a few she had never thought existed. Even if she would never be able to have a dragon of her very own, just being able to touch one, once, would be reward enough for her patience.

2

Aya had wanted a dragon for as long as she could remember. They consumed her thoughts, day and night. She would see members of the elite, mysterious Dragonguard, mounted atop the fabulous beasts that dwarfed their riders in comparison, and her sense of jealousy would be overwhelming. Her emotional response to seeing them was always visceral, something deep down inside her that made her whole body start thrumming with excitement. Something told Aya that she was meant to be among their number, but her life seemed not to reflect that feeling.

Once upon a time, she had shared that excitement with her parents, but her down-to-earth parents quickly knocked down her enthusiasm. After all, why would the Dragonguard want a slip of a girl like her, someone who only had two sets of clothes to her name, and those patched and worn?

Constantly reminded by her father that she was little more than a servant, and only a girl besides, Aya's chances of joining that auspicious company were little to none. It hurt, knowing that was the case. He told her that only the highest ranked, and most privileged of men were given the opportunity to ride a dragon, much less own one. Look at him. He was nearly half a century old and had never gotten within fifty feet of a dragon.

As she had left their small farm fewer than five times in her sixteen years of life, and then only to the closest village, Aya had had far less experience with the world than he had, so he must know something she did not. At least, that is what he often reminded her.

Determined to prove him wrong, to show she was both clever and worthy, Aya had searched the forest for hours on end for dragon eggs. But she never found any, to her great disappointment. Aya wondered where a dragon would lay her eggs, or even if they laid eggs at all, as she had once seen a harmless, shiny, black and green snake by the pond, giving birth to dozens of exquisite little miniatures of herself on the shore, before slipping back into the concealment of the algae-rich primordial broth.

The resident snakes ate the frogs and tadpoles that might otherwise overrun the pond, and the snakes sometimes fed the hawks and owls who often glided soundlessly over the surface of the crops, ever vigilant for the unwary rodent that had strayed too far from its burrow.

Reptiles must be a tasty alternative to rodents, Aya thought, but that did not make her at all curious about how they tasted. She would leave that sort of culinary curiosity to the raptors. Then her mind wandered into wondering what the dragons ate. Whatever it was, it must be substantial.

An entire bullock, perhaps? And then, how often? Were they like snakes, who only ate once every few days, and spent the time in between laying out in the hot sun? Or did they need to eat daily? She hoped she might one day have the opportunity to ask that question and get an answer that had real knowledge behind it.

Aya's father had told her to accept her lot in life, as that was the way things were, but she refused to accept his assertion. She was 16 years old, now only a year or two from some an arranged marriage, which she also did not want either. She wanted exploration and adventure, not a home to which she would be tied for the rest of her life. Hungry mouths to feed and clothes to wash.

She had recently heard her parents discussing her marriage prospects, late at night, when they thought she was asleep. Her parents were fortunate enough to have their sleeping chamber, instead of sharing the main room with their children. Unfortunately for them, as the cottage was not very large, every little noise would grab one's attention, and such an expectation of privacy was unreasonable.

Almost without exception, the candidates she had heard her parents discuss were older men, some of whom already had children from wives who had passed on, and she did not want to be a mother to children who were old enough to be her siblings. Nor had she any desire to play nursemaid to a husband in his dotage. Her father seemed more focused on securing a lucrative match, rather than his daughter's future happiness, while her mother seemed more concerned with Aya's prospects for that happiness.

Aya knew that while her parents discussed her marriage prospects together, it would be her father's decision who she married, and then he would finalize those arrangements. Her mother had not married for love but had been one of many daughters to a townsman with two young sons. When Andagebi's father had approached Hadabeni with an offer to take young Zoraya off his hands, Aya's grateful grandfather, no fool he, had leaped at the opportunity.

She wondered what her father would offer as her dowry to her future husband's family. Theirs was not a wealthy family, and what little they had was necessary for the running of their small farm. Perhaps a ham or two, or even a live hog. She knew her worth to her father.

All Aya wanted was a dragon on which she could fly away from all of that, secure in knowing that she was tied no longer to the land, but had become one with the air itself. It would not even matter if it were male or female if it took her away from the life she now led. How wonderful it must be to fly so high above everyone and everything. She could think of nothing else she desired more. Maybe she would find an egg one day that would successfully hatch out a great beast, but she had begun to believe she would never have that chance. She became convinced that she would grow old and die, forced to tend her future husband's farm and brood.

Heaving a great sigh, Aya picked up the basket of small brown eggs from the top of the fencepost and went inside.

3

"Thank you for bringing in the eggs, Aya," said her mother, Zoraya, as the girl placed the battered old woven reed basket atop the kitchen table. It never ceased to amaze Aya that her mother always seemed to know what was going on around her, without having to look. Indeed, she had not even turned around from the fire, over which she was tending the contents of their precious, but well-worn, iron cookpot. "Please put them in the cool cupboard. I don't know when I will be using them."

"The Dragonguard were out again, Mama," she told her mother, excitement coloring her tone. She heard Zoraya sigh and regretted her words. Even now, Aya would forget herself and blurt out the wrong thing. This was one of those "wrong things."

"I know you covet one for yourself, daughter, and perhaps I understand, but please keep your observations to yourself when your father is near. You know such talk only upsets him," Zoraya told Aya without turning to look at her daughter. "You should be old enough by now to know that avoiding beatings is for the best."

"Yes, Mama," Aya replied, crestfallen that her mother had cut her short.

The smells from the iron pot caught her attention, inside and out. Whatever was in that pot smelled very tasty.

Aya's stomach growled at her as she put the eggs away. Tonight's supper would not be a bland or spare one that much was certain. It would be a welcome change from the scanty meals of the past few days before her brother Gebi had made the long-postponed journey to the closest village for the supplies they lacked.

Already a shrewd bargainer, Gebi took only the best of their produce and goods with him for sale and barter. When he returned, Gebi had most of what he had been sent to obtain, along with a few coppers and silvers.

He had also taken the last pup from their old dog's litter, a sizeable brindle female, and Aya's favorite, and traded her for a few yards of coarse-woven brown cloth. She was not sure yet if she should treasure or hate whatever was made from it.

"Hopefully the hens will feel inspired and lay a few more eggs overnight," her mother said, as she gently stirred the contents of the pot, either not hearing Aya's gastric complaint, or choosing to ignore it. Most likely the latter. Zoraya knew very well that her daughter had not eaten since breakfast. The yeasty aroma of baking bread that still hung in the air added to the maddening aroma of the cottage's interior.

"Oh, the black hen is ready for the stew pot, I think, Mama," Aya replied. "I left her in the coop until you are ready for her. She hasn't laid an egg for at least two weeks now."

"Do it first thing tomorrow morning, and I will be able to stew the meat all day long. It is the only way to make an old hen edible, you know," Zoraya said. "I do not know why you waited this long."

A compliment from her mother would have been nice, but Zoraya seemed incapable of that. Aya had not assumed, and that should have meant something to her, she thought. Aya had gotten into trouble for making such decisions on her own in the past, and knew better than to do it again.

Yes, Aya did know how to cook an old hen, as she had borne the duty of the slaughtering of crippled and barren hens for at least the past six years. Mother rarely dirtied herself anymore with the messy, unpleasant chores, preferring to set her daughter to those tasks, and staying indoors as much as possible. Zoraya's skin, once as pale as her daughter's was now, while she was still young, had long ago turned wrinkled, dark brown and leathery from long days working outside in the kitchen garden, the damage already was done.

"We cannot afford to keep feeding hens who don't lay," her mother muttered, half under her breath. "No sense in wasting good food, after all."

Aya refrained from reminding her mother that the hens fended for themselves when it came to food, as saying anything would only have gotten her into trouble. It was how they kept the grubs and other insects out of their tidy little kitchen garden. Those rich little treats resulted in brilliant yellow yolks that burst in your mouth with rich goodness when you devoured them whole.

All of their hens were on the elderly side, and they were either going to have to buy new hen chicks at the market or get a rooster and hope the hens were fertile enough to lay viable eggs. Again, though, this was not something Aya could bring up to her mother. She only knew that there were going to be at least seven chicken stews in her future.

"Is there anything I can do to help with tonight's supper, Mama," she asked politely, hoping as she always did, that there would be nothing for her. Hope took that moment to fly away.

"Yes, there is. Wash your hands, twice, and then peel the turnips for me after you fetch the small ale barrel from the cellar. Your father and brother should be back in soon, and I would like to have supper ready for the table when they return."

Her mother still had not turned around from the fireplace. The soft, dull scrape of the long wooden spoon against the inside of the pot was soothing and almost hypnotic in its regularity.

"Don't dawdle, child. Be quick about it!"

So much for going outside again to watch for more dragons.

Soon, Aya was scrubbing and then peeling four sizeable turnips. Once she had removed the purple and white skins, she diced them small and threw them into the pot. Aya thriftily saved the turnip peels for the morning's hog slops. Always a thrifty person, nothing went to waste if Aya had a hand in things.

After making certain there was nothing else her mother needed, Aya took the time to wash her face and comb out her long platinum blonde hair before plaiting it into a single long, thick braid that hung to just below her waist. She would need to get up early in the morning to give her hair a good wash, but for now, it was acceptable. She treasured the comb that her brother had carved for her from a cow's rib bone a few winters ago. It had been his Winter Solstice gift to her that year, and she kept it in the hide sheath he had also made that year for her to store it safely.

Father and Gebi, both filthy from the day's labor, came in about an hour later when the stew in the cookpot was boiling merrily once more, and most of the finely chopped turnips had fallen apart enough to thicken the rich broth.

It was a late fall stew, which was always a favorite for Aya. Such a stew in their home was unusual, and Aya wondered what might have happened for this occasion to arise. She hoped it had nothing to do with her.

Mother only served this kind of stew on the night of the winter solstice, and they were at least two months away from that auspicious evening. Aya had already been helping her mother with the annual ritual of turning the current year's collection of old candle drippings into new candles for that event.

Father would soon be slaughtering all of the hogs, except his best sow, and hanging the resulting meat up to smoke, to preserve it for use during the otherwise barren winter months. Mother would turn the fat into large batches of lard that they would use over the next six months to a year. The crisp cracklings that were a by-product of the lard-rendering process would make for a tasty winter snack as well.

4

Mother had banked the fire to keep the stew from burning. There was enough of it that Aya knew she would have it for breakfast the next morning. That would be a very welcome change from their normal morning serving of bland porridge. Mother always served the porridge thin, the way her father preferred it. It was better than nothing, but the operative word was "nothing."

"Take your seat, Aya," Zoraya said, surprising her daughter. "I will take care of serving tonight's supper."

Andagebi and her brother, already seated, had not bothered to wash up first. Their faces were grubby with dust and wheel grease, their fingers filthy and blackened by the day's work. Zoraya placed a steaming towel on the table beside each man, and they used them to wipe as much of the grime from their hands and fingers as possible.

After slicing one of the two fresh loaves of dark bread she had baked that morning into thick slabs, and placing each on its wooden platter, Zoraya ladled up a large helping of thick stew onto each slab, before setting each platter down on the table. Aya eyed her serving eagerly, impatient for the end of the nightly meal invocation. In addition to the turnips she had contributed to the meal, the steaming ladleful of stew before her looked to contain rich-tasting mutton, onion, carrots, winter squash, and some greens, in addition to whatever spices Zoraya had seen fit to add.

She watched greedily as her thick trencher soaked up the hot juices of the stew, and when she was permitted to do so, Aya devoured her supper as though she were starving, down to the very last sodden piece of bread. So efficient was she that nothing was left on her wooden platter but a slight shine of moisture.

Supper was always a mostly silent event, as far as voices were concerned, at least while they all ate. Instead, there was only the sound of chewing and swallowing, as supper was tucked away down hungry gullets.

Wiping his lips with his sleeve, Aya's father Andagebi cleared his throat to gain everyone's attention. His second favorite time of day had begun. After supper was when most announcements were made, and discussions occurred.

"We will begin butchering the hogs tomorrow, Gebi," he began. "The weather will begin to turn soon, and I don't want to be doing it while the snow falls."

"Yes, father," Gebi responded obediently. "I'll see to the knife and hatchet blades tonight."

"Good lad. I want to be up before cock's crow to start. We'll keep the sow, of course, and the biggest speckled barrow."

Aya wondered why Andagebi even said that, as foxes had taken the rooster an age ago, and there was not another within leagues. She wisely kept her thoughts to herself.

Andagebi prattled on about minor things until his words became a blur in Aya's ears. Her father's need to talk until her ears were exhausted frustrated her. She allowed her thoughts to wander, until, suddenly, her father slapped the table, hard.

He gave a broad smile to his family. He seemed quite pleased with himself, and whatever it was he was about to share. Had she missed something important in his earlier monologue?

"An excellent meal, wife," he began. His gaze swept the table. "A fine meal for a night of celebration!"

A celebration? What was this?

"First, Gebi, we will be holding your Naming ceremony in the next few weeks. I have engaged the village clerk to come and witness it and record it in the Great Book."

Aya's brother had been called Gebi since he was an infant, and would not take his adult name until he was deemed an adult. It seemed that time had come, and she wondered what his adult name would be. Indeed, she wondered what hers would be when that time came for her. There was no set naming convention, but firstborns often took their child name from the parent whose gender they shared.

Gebi looked very pleased with his father's words and preened when his father slapped him companionably on the shoulder. Not given to demonstrations of anything resembling affection, this was something to enjoy, for as long as it might last. He caught up a large spoonful of the thick stew, grinning from ear to ear as he did so.

Aya seemed to be the only one who noticed as Zoraya got up, took an overstuffed pie from the top shelf of the kitchen cupboard, and set it down on the table in front of her father, placing a serving utensil next to it. Molten berry juice had bubbled through the slits Zoraya had cut into the top crust, staining the golden brown pastry that capped the pie pink.

A sweet dessert, in addition to the otherwise fine meal? What else was on the surprise horizon tonight? Andagebi cut four servings of pie from the pan and passed them out before continuing, licking sticky pink juice and crumbs from his fingers with obvious relish.

"Now then, on to even larger things, Gebi! With the giving of your adult name, I have also found a wife for you! The eldest daughter of the village clerk is of marrying age, and I have agreed to a marriage contract between you and her."

After taking an enormous bite of his pie wedge, Andagebi splashed some of the weak ale from the ale barrel into each mug at the table, and then raised his to Aya's brother in an odd sort of salute.

His laden spoon halfway to his mouth, Gebi froze, staring at his father. This was a surprise for him. Aya wondered how her parents had kept it from him, as he spent most of his daylight hours with his father. Then she remembered how father had ostensibly gone to the next farm over for some errand or other and had been "forced" to stay the night while the blacksmith there had fixed whatever needed attention.

"A wife? I am to have a wife?" His fork dropped from his fingers and back down onto the waiting trencher.

It was clear to Aya that this announcement had been the reason for the unusually festive meal they had just devoured. She felt her stomach's contents begin to sour.

"Yes, my son, her name is Lorisani," father said in a soft tone at odds with his normal demeanor. "She will arrive, with her dowry, three days hence. Tomorrow, we will begin building an addition onto our home where you and she will sleep."

Her brother stared into the middle distance, eyes unfocused.

"A wife?" Gebi could not seem to get past the idea that he was being married off. Aya was reminded of a rabbit surprised by torches in the night. It seemed to her that he did not appear pleased at the notion. Why would that be? Did he not want a family of his own?

Mother burst into tears, but Aya's father affected not to notice her unhappiness. Her son was no longer her little boy, but a grown man who would now have a woman of his own. Aya wondered how her mother would feel once her daughter's engagement was announced. Would she mourn her daughter's absence for love, or because her handmaiden was no longer in residence? Then she mentally slapped herself for having such an uncharitable thought.

Father gave Gebi another comradely slap on the shoulder and grinned at him. Aya was an uncomfortable spectator. Gebi seemed only slightly less uncomfortable.

"Soon you'll be working on a fine pack of grandsons for me!" Aya's father enthused. Leave it to Andagebi to think of the marriage as a way to increase his wealth. "With more strong backs to work the fields, we'll double or even triple the harvest!"

Aya wondered how large the dowry had been, as Loris was one of several daughters in that family, and certainly not the oldest of them.

Zoraya continued to cry silently. Unable to watch, Aya rose from her chair and began collecting the dirty platters and utensils from the table. She left everything at Gebi's place alone. He would, she imagined, finish everything there before he rose from his place, but with the news, it might take him some time to accomplish that.

She was halfway to the kitchen counter when her father spoke again. His voice was nowhere near as jovial and self-congratulatory as it had been when he spoke of Gebi's engagement.

"Next we shall see about getting you married off, my daughter." His voice sounded cold to her ears. Aya heard her mother gasp. This news, it seemed, was a surprise to her as well.

Aya froze and then turned around, surely looking as shocked as her brother had only a few moments earlier. She felt tears beginning to brim and fought to keep from rubbing them away. It would only lead to more tears.

"Husband, she is too young yet for marriage," her mother broke in, wiping her own eyes with the hem of her threadbare apron. "Not for at least another year!"

Aya watched as Father glanced at her mother, raising an eyebrow. Aya braced herself for an explosion.

"At least a year? The baker— ".

An expression of horror crossed Zoraya's face.

"Branathar the baker has his choice of many fine girls," she blurted, her voice wavering a bit. "Unless he is willing to wait a year, he *cannot* have Aya."

"Cannot?" Andagebi's question came out as a low growl.

"No," Zoraya replied with unaccustomed determination.

"Three women in the same home? That is more than any man should have to bear." Her father had never considered what his life might have been like if her mother had borne more than a single daughter. "She will be at her most fertile now, and I have assured Branathar that she will produce many fine sons for him. Look at those nice, wide, childbearing hips. I could wish as much for my heifers!"

Zoraya gasped again, and Aya felt sick to her stomach at her father's words. He made her sound like one of the livestock.

"She is still too small to have children, husband! She needs more time to grow!" Desperation tinged her voice as she pleaded with Andagebi. Aya could see the storm brewing in her father's eyes.

"Nonsense, woman! You were younger than she was when you had Gebi! You did just fine, carrying him to term. A fine, healthy boy. You have never had troubles with any of your pregnancies."

"You are taking my son from me, Andagebi," Zoraya said to her husband angrily, her tears drying on her cheeks. "Do not take my daughter from me hot on the heels of that loss. It is only another year, husband."

"My father and his father before him worked this land, Zoraya. I need my son and grandsons by my side, planting, and tending and harvesting. Not some worthless female," he spat, his cheeks awash in a lurid blush. He slid a lewd glance over to his only daughter as he spewed his venom.

Aya tried, unsuccessfully, not to cringe at his harsh words, and saw Andagebi's ghost of a smile at her reaction. "It is bad enough that I have to provide a suitable dowry to get her married off. I am not a wealthy man, after all."

"Surely another year will not put us in the poorhouse, Andagebi!" her mother interjected. "I need her here to help me with the chores!"

"Gebi's new wife will take her place, Zoraya. I am sure that if she is not already trained, I will be able to accomplish that task quickly enough." Father stared hard at her mother as he spoke, and Aya could see the anger rising in his eyes. "You will not lose a servant, wife. You will gain strong grandsons out of Lorisani."

"Aya knows how to coax the hens into laying more eggs, Andagebi! Even I do not know how she manages to do that. The hens are old, and will soon stop laying altogether."

Mother rarely raised her voice against father, and he was startled and angry that she had done so now. Father always said that while the king ruled the country, he was king in his home, and her mother's outburst ran against this tradition. He rose from his seat, his hand going to the worn leather belt around his waist.

"Then she can teach Lorisani that secret before she goes to wed the baker, Zoraya. It cannot be that difficult a thing to accomplish if even a girl can do it."

Both Aya and her brother were on intimate terms with that leather strap and its horrid iron buckle. While the leather of that belt left red raised welts that would eventually heal cleanly, the buckle would sometimes cut into bare flesh, leaving permanent scars behind in its wake. She had never seen her father use it on her mother but knew that did not mean he had never used it outside of her presence.

"Aya, my daughter, go clean the platters. You don't want the food to dry on them and make them harder to clean," her mother said, keeping her voice steady as she stared back at her husband, defiance clear in her expression. As Aya slipped out the door, she heard her father's voice raise in anger.

"How dare you say such a thing in front of the children, Zoraya? You are never again to undermine — "

Aya managed to get far enough away that she could not hear the rest of whatever it was her father said. She was not so far away, though, that she did not hear a loud crash come from inside their small home. Grabbing the pumping mechanism, Aya began to pump water from the well into the waiting bucket, the squealing sound it made helping to dull the other loud noises that came from the interior of the cottage.

Married? So soon? She had no desire to be married, yet her father was already making the arrangements! It was all she could do not to cry.

Once cool enough, fresh water was in the bucket, and Aya was scrubbing the cracked and worn platters clean, she began to wonder why her mother, who she had heard participating not reluctantly in marriage conversations with her father, was suddenly so against trying to marry her off. Gebi's new wife would take her place on the chore front once he was married, so she had nothing to worry about on that score.

Aya tried to remember if the clerk's oldest daughter seemed a biddable girl, the very few times she had laid eyes on her. All she could remember was that the girl was dark skinned, with dark, curly hair, and dark eyes, and did not speak many more words than was necessary for a conversation.

Of course, being quiet did not immediately translate to obedience. Lorisani could simply be biding time before escaping the family home. Aya had seen that before. Either way, it probably would not be long before her father broke the girl's spirit. He did not want spunk; he wanted obedience.

She was startled out of her reverie when she heard her father call her name. His voice was still angry, and Aya was afraid of what that anger would mean for her. He could not see her from the doorway, so neither could she see him, but his voice still frightened her to her bones.

Would her father commit violence upon her with the Dragonguard overhead? Her eyes swept the sky, as she prayed for the sudden appearance of dragons, but saw none. Would it have mattered if they had been there? Would they have noticed or even cared? Were domestic issues beyond their realm of concern?

If only she were a Dragonguard, it would be one of hers.

"Aya! Daughter! Come here now!" Andagebi's tone was still tight with anger.

Clutching the stack of wooden platters to her chest like an impromptu shield, Aya made her way around the corner, where he would be able to see her from the cottage, but would not be so close as to be able to grab her. He had grabbed her before, for unexpected beatings.

Aya saw what appeared to be blood on the front of his tunic, and stopped moving. Three long bloody scratches ran down one cheek, blood drooling down his neck and onto the filth-stained garment. Mother, it seemed, had not taken her beating meekly. Good for her.

"Aya, come here, now," he told her, his voice at a deadly quiet level. His belt dangled from his hand, and Aya wondered if it did not now seem darker than it had been before he removed it earlier. She obediently began to walk toward him, but her pace was slow. At the last possible moment, he stepped away and pointed at the cottage behind him. "Your mother wants you."

"Yes, father," she replied, still not moving, and watched him as he walked away from the cottage in the general direction of the south field, away from her. She hoped he would be gone a long while, or at least long enough to lose his anger.

What had he done to her mother that required Aya's assistance? What would she find when she entered the cottage? Dread filled her.

Only once he was far enough away that he did not pose a threat did she begin to walk toward the cottage. The small farm seemed oddly quiet, as though even the livestock waited to discover what lay inside the darkened building.

"Gebi! Where are you, boy?" her father shouted.

Andagebi had walked away without a backward glance, their old dog keeping close to his heels, making Aya wondered where her brother might have gone, and if he was far enough away that he could not hear his father calling his name.

5

O nce she reached the cottage and went back inside, Aya gasped in horror. Her mother was on the floor, face down in a puddle of spoiled ale that had emptied from its shattered barrel. She was covered in blood and not moving, except for the slight rise and fall of her back as she breathed. Fragments of the now destroyed berry pie were splattered across her mother, the table, and the floor.

Aya was afraid to come any closer, fearing what she would find when she did. Zoraya's breathing was shallow, not strong, and that frightened her.

It looked as though Gebi had left the cottage via the front door, as he was nowhere in sight. Coward. So that was why her father had wandered off. She hoped he would be gone a long time, in his search for her weasel of a brother.

"Mama?"

There was no answer, nor any change in her breathing.

Gathering her courage and moving to her mother's side, Aya carefully rolled Zoraya over and saw that her father had brutally beaten her. Aya felt sick inside when she realized that her mother's nose was now a flattened wreck. Andagebi had not pulled his punches.

"Oh, Mama!" was all Aya could say. The awful wounds on her mother's face would probably leave ugly scars behind. The one mirror they possessed, which was little better than a sheet of polished metal, would maybe be blurry enough to conceal the damage that Andagebi had left behind, as it was far from perfect. Perhaps that was a blessing.

She wet an almost-clean rag and used it to wash the blood from her mother's face gently, and then did what she could to stem the bleeding of her mother's once delicate nose. She had no idea of what she could do to fix it, so she simply took another clean rag, wet it down as well, and laid it gently against her mother's nostrils. It broke her heart to know it would not heal well.

Mother's eyes fluttered open ever so slightly, and Aya saw her gaze fix on her. Ugly bruises were already beginning to form around her mother's eyes, made to look even worse in the flickering light of the fire.

"Aya, my daughter, what are you doing here? Why did you not flee when I told you to go outside?"

Aya was surprised by her mother's question. Where else would she be?

"I'm here because father told me to come and tend to you, Mama. If I had known he would do this to you, I would not have left the house."

Zoraya frowned, and then winced as the expression tugged at skin and muscles damaged by the beating Andagebi had administered

"I wanted to keep you safe, Aya, and that has not changed. Your father is intent on marrying you to the baker, child. I have heard too many terrible things about him to permit such a thing to come to pass," her mother whispered weakly. "So many terrible things."

"What can I do about that, Mama? I have nowhere else to go."

Her mother seemed to come back to herself and focused on her daughter once more. She reached out a hand and squeezed her daughter's upper arm.

"I have a small bag of coins in the back of the grain cupboard, Aya. I want you to take them and my jewelry, which your father planned to use as your dowry, anyway, and go. Go far away. Perhaps you can find yourself a kind husband out somewhere in the world, away from the murderous baker."

"Murderous?"

"His last wife died under questionable circumstances, Aya," her mother told her. "Stop wasting time. Put on your warmest clothes, grab the bag of coins and my jewelry, take some food, and flee while you can. He plans to send you to Branathar the baker in the morning."

A chill thrilled through Aya's spine, and she did as she was bid, stopping only to help her mother into a sitting position against the table's leg, wrap her mother's worn shawl around her mother's skinny shoulders, and to give her a farewell kiss. The trio of plain, thin, gold bracelets her mother had given her knocked against one another with a slight jangling sound.

"I am glad you will have those, Aya. My mother, your grandmother, gave them to me when I married your father. Better that you have them for yourself, rather than some man's family, who would not appreciate their stories. There is something else you must know before you leave if only to impress upon you why you should go and never come back."

Aya just looked at her mother.

"He murdered your infant sisters when I did not bear him another son. I will not lose you as well," Zoraya murmured, and coughed thickly, bringing up dark red blood when she did. "He took them while I slept and did away with them both."

"Sisters? I had sisters?" She remembered her father's words about her mother's pregnancies, as though she had had more than two, and felt as though she would vomit. "Where are they? What happened to them?"

"They are long gone, my dear Aya. Now you must be long gone as well before your father returns. I would see you safely away from here. Take the youngest hen and the old black hen with you when you go. One will give you eggs, perhaps, and you can eat the other. *He* does not need them."

She pushed her daughter away from her, weakly, but not unkindly.

"I have always loved you, my dear Aya. I am sorry that I did not say it more often. You have grown into a fine young woman, and I am proud of you. Good fortune to you, my daughter," her mother said, as Aya left. "I will always be with you, wherever you may go in life."

6

Aya set the livestock loose before she left. She knew that it would take precious time to round them all up again, as the dog was old, and not as limber as she had once been, so it would delay any pursuit by her father and brother, who would not risk losing any of the precious animals to the forest and the wolves within. She wished them all well in their bid for freedom, however long that freedom might last.

The hogs and cows were elated at their unexpected escape and made the most of it. The six hogs promptly wandered into the nearby melon field, happily devouring the ripe, unharvested bounty that lay on the ground. After being shooed out of their pen, the cows contented themselves by meandering toward the half-grown barley field. The cows only rarely hurried, and this was not one of those times.

She took the thin golden bracelets off her wrist and tucked them away safely in the pack she carried on her back. There was no sense in drawing any more attention to herself with the gaudy bangles. Her mother had come from a family that, while not wealthy, was reasonably well-off. Her mother's gift would be good for barter, should circumstances become so dire that she needed to exchange them for food or clothing. She knew very little about from whence her mother had come, as Zoraya had shared little of her childhood, to keep her daughter from feeling as deprived as she.

Her mother's family had lived in a town, rather than on a farm, but with four daughters to marry off, Aya's grandfather had arranged for whatever marriages he could, as four dowries might very well bankrupt a man, if he was not a shrewd bargainer.

Zoraya was the oldest daughter, so hers had been the first dowry he had provided. Had Grandmother Izanaya saved back other bits of her jewelry for her younger daughters, as they had been sent off to their new homes? Aya did not know.

Aya had met her maternal grandmother once, and the old woman, widowed and living with her youngest daughter, Izaorna and her family, had gabbled on incessantly about how she was so disappointed that her beloved daughter had been reduced to the position of scullery maid. Andagebi had sent the old woman on her way as soon as he was able.

Tears ran down Aya's cheeks as she ran for the safety of the forest, and she wondered if the Dragonguard would have interceded on behalf of her mother, had they known she was being beaten. On the other hand, was such mundane intercession something they avoided? She determined to ask one of them when the opportunity presented itself, should she be so lucky as to meet a Dragonguard.

Aya was nearly to the edge of the forest, the two hens fussing quietly in the burlap sack she had strapped to her back when she became aware of an odd glow behind her. Turning, she saw the cottage, engulfed in flames, and with a surge of grief, knew that her mother would no longer need anyone to do chores for her. Perhaps Zoraya knew that her injuries were far greater than could be seen, and this was her revenge on her husband for inflicting them upon her.

Andagebi's fury would be terrible, and the loss of his home might very well cancel Gebi's engagement as well. Better to be far away from that explosion. Perhaps her brother would be caught in that fire, for a change.

As she had been playing in the forest since the time she was old enough to walk, Aya did not find it to be a threatening place. Over the years, she had even found places where she would conceal herself all day long, hiding from Gebi, who enjoyed tormenting his little sister. The wolves, seeming to sense a kindred spirit, had watched from a distance, but left her alone. Knowing that being in their good graces was not a bad idea, she would bring scraps for them on those days she could sneak away with something she felt a wolf would consider tasty. Bones were a frequent offering to her lupine hosts.

Aya knew the forest was ancient, as some of its trees seemed to touch the sky itself. Other trees were so old, they had hollowed out centers, and only a crust of bark remained as a great cavern to show that a tree had ever stood in its place. Aya imagined the gods and fair folk gathering there for councils of war. It was clear to her that dragons had never thought to lay eggs in such splendid places.

The egg basket, with its meager offering of a half dozen oblong treasure chests, dangled from one hand, while the other hand grasped a stout walking stick. A second burlap sack lay alongside the bag that held the hens, heavy with what small items Aya was capable of carrying with her in her flight.

She had put some of the leftover stew into the single undamaged stoneware container the family owned and then sealed it with a scrap of oiled leather, and a piece of twine. It was enough to last until breakfast, two days hence, provided she was careful with how much she ate. The loaf of bread she had taken with her would help to fill up those bits she would not be able to fill with stew. Hopefully, the young hen would oblige her with an egg or two, providing it was not too stressed from travel. The black hen would live a bit longer, at least until Aya absolutely could not avoid eating her.

Aya was angry that Gebi had left their mother to be beaten by their father, but he was a reflection of his father. He had been raised to believe that the male head of the house had final say in everything, and the law had no rules against beating wives and girl children, even to the point of death. It was grossly unfair, but that was life, as she knew it.

She had thought to take some dried meat from the storehouse when she left so she would have that to nibble on after the stew and bread were gone. Andagebi would be outraged when he discovered that at least five pounds of dried meat were missing, but she would be long gone by the time he did.

Even with the preparations she had made, Aya knew that she could not spend the rest of her life hiding in the forest so she would have to find somewhere else to live.

That would mean not in the nearby village, as she was known there, and that was where the villainous baker appeared to be making ready for her to be his next wife. Even two villages over would be too close to her father and brother, Aya knew so she would need to plan on a significant journey to get to a place where no one knew her.

7

She remained in the forest, high up in the branches of her favorite tree until she had finished the stew and the bread, and her tears would no longer come. Long ago, she had built a shelter of sorts in those high branches, where she had hidden some of the bits and bobs of her childhood. It had become a familiar place to her and seemed a good place to conceal herself, as Gebi and Andagebi had never known about it. Certainly, neither would think to look for her in such a place.

The young hen, which she decided to call Freckles, laid a few eggs during that time, and Aya swallowed them raw, so as not to draw attention to herself with the glow or smoke of a fire. The black hen remained nameless, as Aya did not want to create the emotional attachment a name could bring.

She cried for her mother, and the sisters she had never known. This new information about what might have been made the bloom of hatred that lay in her heart for her father become a poisonous thorn bush. At one point, she heard her father nearby, angrily calling out her name, but he did not know of her current hiding place, so he did not find her.

Amused at the sight, Aya was able to watch him blunder through the rotting leaves and fallen logs, and he eventually went back in the direction of the ruins of her former home. Afraid that the chickens might reveal her presence, Aya had put both birds back into the burlap sack and wrapped it snugly around them, knowing that the sudden darkness and restriction would keep them from being noisy.

She suspected that Gebi had accompanied his father into the forest, and had concealed himself nearby when Andagebi left, hoping to catch his sister and return her to their father for whatever punishment he deemed fit. She did not relish the idea of having to wait him out, but with Fortune's blessing, a rescue of sorts arrived within a few hours.

The wolves, who were never far away, caught either her scent or that of her brother and came to investigate. They must have moved with stealth, as she heard a deep growl, a startled exclamation from her brother, and then the sound of him racing away as fast as his legs would carry him.

It was plain to Aya that the wolves were only playing with Gebi, as they did not attack him, but only chased him off. They usually fed well off the deer that also called the forest home, and she imagined that they were more concerned about chasing off a fellow predator than eating one. She was glad they had never played similar games with her during her visits to their territory.

Eventually, the time came when she said goodbye to the ancient tree that had sheltered her. She had decided to keep moving through the forest, to see where that direction would take her. It would certainly be better than staying anywhere near her childhood home. She could hear the wolves around her, but they never approached. Perhaps she was not "predator" enough to concern them, and for that, she was grateful.

It took Aya nearly a week to make her way through the thickly forested land, sleeping high in the trees to keep the curious wolves at bay, to a place she had never before laid eyes upon, nor heard of in the stories, often embellished, that her father would often tell of his travels. She kept to herself as much as possible, hiding when she heard others near. A woman of any age, out on her own, was considered unacceptable, and it would put her in great danger if she were discovered.

Several days of hard walking later, Aya caught sight of what appeared to be a walled city. Fighting down fears of discovery and a forced return to her father's farm, she decided to go to it and see if she could at least find victuals for her continued journey. There was even the chance she might find someone willing to take her in for the winter months, in exchange for housekeeping. She certainly had the experience.

As she stood outside the high stone walls, it quickly became evident that this village was uninhabited, at least by humans, for whatever reason. Curious, though not at all frightened, Aya walked into the abandoned village and looked around, knowing that she had her pick of the surviving buildings, in the absence of their original inhabitants.

Many of the stone buildings within had fallen in upon themselves during their long abandonment, although some still managed to stand reasonably upright. What appeared to be the town's center was filled with what must have once been a rather ornate large building. The cracked fountain in front of the rotting edifice had long since dried up and was now full of weeds and debris.

Only a few of the stained glass windows remained unbroken, and when she ventured inside, she heard the resident vermin run in terror at her intrusion. Aya could not remember the last time she had frightened anyone or anything, so their hasty exit made her smile.

The building had been looted long ago of its obvious treasures, although the shelves set into the walls still held several books or the remains of books. Aya, who had never learned to read, but enjoyed looking at the illustrations, took one down and fingered her way through it, admiring the carefully painted pictures, before carefully putting it back on its shelf.

Having satisfied herself as to its contents, Aya left the building and scouted around for a place to stay. She knew that her father and brother, being superstitious people, would never enter an abandoned town, for fear of "evil spirits" so she would be relatively safe in the town for the time being. She would stay until she had filled her stores at least a little more and then move out once again.

Aya found her safe spot in a back corner in a small cottage that was almost a part of the rear wall of the town. Surprisingly, a small, dented, old cookpot in reasonable repair still hung over the long-cold ashes of the fireplace. It was just what she needed.

The bed she found within had not rotted too badly, and after beating the dust out of the worn mattress it supported and flipping it over, it made a serviceable bed for her. As there were three rooms, she gave one over entirely to the hens. Aya had no plans to stay long enough to need to clean it out again.

She gathered some old wood from the edge of the forest and used that to make as smokeless a fire as she knew how to create, to stay warm during the cooling nights and to make what food she could for herself from what she had managed to gather during the daylight hours.

Using simple snares, Aya caught hares, squirrels, and the occasional bird, and made use of every part of their carcasses as she was able, devouring the cooked birds, and then smoking and drying the hare and squirrel meat. She cured the small mammals' hides and used them to make a crude fur-lined cloak for herself. It would win no beauty contests, but by the time she was done with it, the day the first snows fell, it was a warm and welcome addition to her wardrobe. She was glad that her brother had charmed her into working the hides that he took when he was out hunting, else she would never have learned how to do it for herself now.

The badly wounded deer she found early one morning and put out of its misery provided an unexpected windfall in food and the opportunity to tan a decent-sized hide. She tried to find a way to make as much use of the carcass as possible, not wanting to waste anything if she could avoid it.

Aya had nearly taken every small mammal in her immediate vicinity as she stocked up for the winter months. Between their smoked and dried meat, and the fruits, edible fungi, and vegetables she had managed to collect before the first freeze made them inedible, she knew she should do reasonably well until perhaps a month after the winter solstice.

She had stacked all the firewood she was able to collect up against the far side of the cottage, where someone randomly coming by would not see it unless they were looking for it. It came to the edge of the roof, and all the way down the length of the cottage, so, if she was wise, and slept under her soft, deer hide lined cloak for additional warmth, it should last her throughout her stay.

The cookpot had required over an hour of hard scrubbing to remove the unidentifiable crusts and rust from its interior, but once it was clean, Aya was pleased with the result. Having it to use made it feel more as though she was home, rather than being a sort of vagabond.

Over time, she moved most of the surviving books and scrolls from the town hall into her snug little cottage, sliding them into the empty shelves that lined the east wall. She felt as though they needed a caretaker, and assumed that mantle on their behalf.

One of the scrolls had revealed a map, although Aya did not know how current it might be. It seemed to show the village and the great forest though, and roads leading to the east and west, with the village shown in its center. Assuming it showed correct information, Aya decided to use it as her guide, when the time came that she moved on.

Everything was fine the first six weeks or so after the snows began to fall, but one morning, Aya awoke with a clogged, snotty nose, and a tremendous headache that made it nearly impossible to open her eyes, the brightness of the light against the snow hurt her eyes so badly.

The old black hen had died two days earlier when it was attacked by a starving weasel that had found a way into the otherwise snug cottage, and Aya had barely been able to retrieve as much of the bird's carcass as she had. Forced into action by this tragedy, Aya had turned the ragged corpse into a meat broth. She took advantage of an unexpected pair of not-yet-shelled eggs she found inside the hen while gutting the thing as a tasty treat to add to the soup.

The thieving weasel's hide had been set to dry, near the sparse fire she kept. At least the beast had not been able to reach the more productive and younger Freckles, who had flapped up to an inset shelf in one wall and waited there, safe and sound, as the older bird, unable to flap one of her wings, had died.

A small amount of broth remained in the cooking pot, so she ladled it out carefully and drank it down, enjoying the thick richness of it all. Then, dipping into her precious water supply, she started a new pot of soup, using some of her dried meat and a few of the root vegetables she had dug up before the snow fell.

She knew it would have tasted better with salt, but she had to settle for using only the herbs she had managed to collect, including the surprising discovery of a small hot pepper bush, whose fruits burned her tongue, but which added so much more excitement to what would have otherwise been bland fare.

The illness lasted nearly a week, during which time she heard activity outside her small hideaway. Unhappily, she banked her fire to conceal her presence and waited in the cooling cottage, wrapped up in every bit of clothing she possessed to stay warm until the sounds of the interloper went away. The last thing she wanted was some fool bringing her back to her father, or worse, to the baker.

Aya was sick of soup to her very bones by the time the illness passed. She would have consumed more solid fare, but her mother had taught Aya that soups were best when one was ill, and she had never forgotten that lesson.

From time to time, Aya would indulge in a long bout of crying for her mother. She felt ashamed that she had ever felt that her mother loved her brother more than her. It was clear that her mother had only her best interests in mind when the end came. That thought just brought on more tears, and Aya was surprised that she did not simply wither up and dry out from as much as she cried.

While she waited for the snows to recede, Aya planned what she would do, once she left the not-so-abandoned village. She knew she needed to find some civilization, as she could not live the life of a nomad forever, and did not want to.

8

Bored from being stuck inside for several days during the snowstorm, Aya took advantage of the first break in the weather to escape from the cottage and do some more exploring of her domain.

Previous forays had resulted in the acquisition of various bits and pieces that made her solitary life in the cottage more bearable. Things that looters seeking treasure might otherwise overlook, as they had no real meaning for them. But for Aya, a wooden spoon, an unbroken mug, a small knife, all of those were of immediate use to her.

They were treasure enough for her when she did not have any of her own when she arrived.

She knew the town hall had been well looted, but curiosity made her head back in to see what she might find that escaped the notice of previous treasure hunters. They had already demonstrated a profound disinterest in the books and scrolls located there, so who knew what else might have been dismissed as lacking value. She would not know until she took the time to look.

There were two stories aboveground to the building, and a basement, from what she had been able to determine. With no windows to the outside world, the basement remained in darkness, unless one brought their light source with them. There were wall sconces down there, but their lamp oil was long since burned away. Aya needed to find an alternative light source before she could assay any exploration of the building's depths.

To that end, Aya had collected and rendered all the fat she could from the carcasses of the animals she trapped and kept it against the day that she had enough to make a decent foray into that foreboding basement. In the absence of wax and tallow, it was all she could use.

Aya soaked strips of rag in the precious melted fat, wrung the excess from them, and then wrapped the fat-impregnated rags around a short, thick branch to be used as a torch. She had learned the trick from her mother, years ago, when they had unexpectedly run out of tallow candles due to the depredations of rats and mice.

With luck, the torchlight would last long enough for her to make a decent foray into the basement. With even better luck, she might find something else that would make her life at least a little bit easier.

The inside of the town hall had become very familiar to her, with her frequent incursions in search of new books and scrolls to admire. She had found the single mug she now possessed lying in a dark corner beneath what must have been the town clerk's desk. Its otherwise brown clay substance was shot through with streaks of some mysterious green clay, adding character to what might otherwise have been something ordinary and otherwise forgettable.

The door to the basement had long ago been broken open, and what little of the door that remained hung limply from the sole iron hinge that barely remained affixed to the door's frame. Aya had gathered the broken and splintered bits of wood from the floor and used them for her fire. It only made sense to take advantage of what was most easily available.

The torch burned with an oily, black smoke, but put out enough light that Aya was able to slowly make her way down the stairway into the depths of the basement.

It provided just enough light to keep her from tripping and falling over the skeletal remains of some unidentifiable person who had never made it back up that stairway and into the light. Whoever it was had been dead a very long time, as the stench of decay was long gone.

What little flesh remained on the body had dried to the point of mummification, its thin lips drawn back from half-rotted teeth in a horrible rictus of a grin.

Aya imagined that however the man had died, it had not been a peaceful passing. The skeleton's posture was not relaxed but suggested some great agony.

Not more than five feet further on, and she discovered two more sets of human remains, although these were no more than skeletons at this late date. What could have happened that would result in such obvious violence?

The flickering light of the rude torch did not illuminate the chamber fully, so Aya's exploration required close inspection of anything she wanted to explore. If the deceased had worn jewelry, it was long gone at this point; either taken by earlier adventurers, or fallen off and tumbled into the shadows as the skeletons slowly lost their cohesion and fell apart.

It was readily apparent that loose bricks had been pulled away from their settings so that the spaces behind could be checked for treasure secreted within. After seeing a fat, well-fed spider tucked inside one of those revealed spaces, Aya was a bit more careful in her exploration.

By the time the torch's flame was becoming more fitful, Aya had explored most of the basement area, and had uncovered nothing that was very helpful to her. She was disappointed, of course, after having gone to the trouble of hoarding fat for the torch, but knew that if she had not done so, so would always regret it.

She misjudged how much time she had left, and so was quite surprised when the torch's flame failed and went out completely, leaving her in the absolute blackness of the chilly underground chamber. It was frightening, and Aya fancied she could hear *things* moving around her in the dark.

Trying to orient herself as to her location, Aya stepped forward and tripped over one of the skeletons at the base of the stairs, falling into it, hard. Fragile bones *crunched* beneath the force of her landing, and Aya felt her gorge rise in response.

When Aya fell, she had instinctively put out her hands and was surprised to find her fingers curled around a slender stick that must have lain beneath the skeleton upon which she had tripped. Keeping it at hand to help feel her way back up the stairs, Aya rose, brushing dust and bone fragments away.

The stick turned out to be just what she needed, and with its aid, was able to make her way back up into the blessed light of day, such as there was, as the sun was now making its descent to the horizon. A light snow was falling, and Aya dashed back to her cottage, not wanting to be out in the cold temperatures any longer than she must.

Over a steaming mug of broth, Aya examined the mysterious stick she had picked up. It was no simple piece of wood, but something more than that, though she had no idea what that something might be.

It was about ten millimeters in diameter, and a meter and a half long. Despite its length, it was very light in Aya's hand, its weight almost negligible. Upon closer inspection, she discovered that it possessed a metal tip on one end, and a metal cap on the other, with a metal collar at its neck that featured a delicate loop that would be perfect for a wrist strap.

With a bit of rubbing, Aya discovered that the metal furnishings seemed to be a kind of silver that was nearly white in color. As she cleared the accumulated grime from the thing, she also found delicate etchings of dragons along its length, flying nose to tail like a magnificent aerial parade. She wondered how anyone could leave such a glorious piece of artwork behind and then realized its past owner could be among the skeletons whose acquaintance she had so recently made.

Aya had no desire to go back into the dark basement, so that would remain a mystery unless, by some twist of fate, she discovered more about it out in the sunlit world. While she was willing to do a lot, she had reached the point where she had had enough.

Using a short, greasy piece of rag that had not been used on the now extinct torch Aya had used in her ill-fated expedition, she rubbed the stick up and down. As she carefully worked, she discovered an almost translucent black object that covered in etchings of dragons, capped and footed with fine silver.

It was clear that the object was not made of wood, as she had never seen translucent wood, but then, it was also too light to be stone, either. The thing felt oddly warm and comfortable in her hand. It felt *right* in her grasp.

9

She had finally slaughtered the remaining hen and was down to her last small stack of dried meat by the time the snows finally began to melt, and her jaws were sore from having to chew through the thick slabs of protein. The vegetables she had so carefully tucked away had been gone for at least a month, and the monotonous fare was taking its toll on her.

Packing everything she could into the carry-sacks she had made with the skins that had not gone into making her cloak, she left the cottage for good on the first day the ground was clear of snow. Aya could not leave it soon enough, as far as she was concerned.

Unable to leave a mess behind, she had taken the time to clear the place of any trash remaining, in the event someone else might need a place to stay in the future. It was her way of saying 'thank you' to what god or gods had put the cottage in her path when she needed a place to stay over the winter months.

She had deliberately dirtied up the surface of the mysterious stick to disguise it, as it would have been too difficult to conceal otherwise, as it was so very long. For now, it appeared to be a well-used walking stick, and in case she needed to defend herself, it would be right at hand.

She began to wonder if other people shunned the abandoned village much as her father and brother would have done. She had lived there for several months and, other than herself, she had only noted one incursion in that time.

Perhaps plague had taken the village and its inhabitants, and by some miracle, she had not contracted it. The plague had taken the only other village she had ever heard of that had ultimately been burned to the ground. The inhabitants, living and dead, had been pushed back into the homes by monitors and the doors boarded up to keep the unfortunate victims from escaping the flames and certain death. Aya determined never to tell anyone she had spent any time in this eerie town.

She pretended to herself that she had not gone back and taken the heavy illustrated volume she had discovered on her first day in the village. While she had enjoyed many of the other books she had scavenged, this one was special to her. It was much too beautiful to leave to rot, and perhaps one day she would learn to read and find out what magic lived within its pages.

Aya had walked for days before she encountered another human being. When she first heard him speak, the unfamiliarity of the experience made her jump.

"And what are you doing out here, all alone, little missy?" said a voice from above. "Not at all normal to see a young woman out on her own in this part of the world."

Squeaking a bit, Aya looked up and saw a blood-red dragon and its rider a short distance from her, hovering silently. The swarthy-faced human grinned down at her, clearly pleased that he had surprised her. She noted in passing that rather than sitting directly on the dragon's hide, the Dragonguard sat atop a large blanket that was spread across the beast's massive shoulders and appeared to have been fastened in place with leather strapping. The blanket was decorated with a simple repeated pattern of swirling lines.

"I'm traveling," she replied stoutly, gesturing vaguely with the stick. "I want to find my way in the world."

"Oh, you do, do you," he asked her, a smirk playing about his lips. "And do you propose to walk wherever that may be?"

"If I must. I do not have a beast to ride, nor anything as grand as a dragon," she dared. "If I had a dragon of my own, I would go wherever I wished!"

"Oh-ho!" the dragonman chortled. "Yes, aim high whenever you can."

The dragon in question snorted at her words, and Aya's eyes widened. Had she said something wrong?

"Don't give him so much praise, little girl," the dragonman said. "It will go to his head, and then I won't be able to do anything with him!"

The dragon snorted again, but this time, it seemed that it was aimed at his rider.

"The dragon understands my words?"

"Of course he does. He does not speak, himself, but does make himself understood."

"I'm sorry if I've offended you, dragon," she told the great beast politely. The dragon landed and folded its great wings at its sides, regarding her with his gigantic blue eyes, which, she saw, were the same color as his rider's. She also noted that the dragon's landing was almost silent. "I did not mean to do so."

The dragon licked at Aya's face, and it was all she could do not to scream and jump backward. Oddly, beast's long, red, forked tongue had been dry, rather than moist, which was unexpected. The Dragonguard laughed.

The dragon made a strange noise, and Aya turned her attention to the rider.

"He's not offended by anything you've said or done, little girl," he replied, an odd expression on his face. "However, I know, and I would think you do not, that there will be more snow overnight, and I do not think you will have a safe place to be when that happens. May I offer you a ride somewhere?"

Aya stammered a response, not sure what she said in reply, but whatever it was, the rider took it as an affirmative, and the dragon reached out a paw to gently pick her up and hand up her to his rider. It was so sudden a movement that Aya did not have a chance to avoid it.

The skin of the dragon's taloned paw felt soft as it closed about her, which was something she had not expected. Aya had always thought of dragons as being hard-scaled, but this was very different.

The next thing she knew, Aya was astride the dragon's broad shoulders, sitting in front of his rider, who looped one arm around her belly to keep her from falling off. There was nothing inappropriate in his grasp, only necessity. She noticed that the arm which held her seemed damaged, and on closer examination, she saw that he was missing some fingers.

Not knowing if asking about it would offend him, she did not ask about the arm.

"Are you comfortable where you are? Here we go!"

With that, the dragon leaped into the air with a massive downbeat of his wings, the action surprisingly smooth for a beast that must easily weigh over three thousand pounds. Aya stared down at the ground, startled by their speed and watching the ground move away at a surprising pace.

"Not afraid of heights? You surprise me, girl," the rider said. "You seem to be very fond of dragons. I'd think you'd be more afraid than excited."

"Aya, not 'girl,'" she told him, offended by his assumption. "My name is Aya. I am not afraid of heights. This is just different for me."

"Aya. Hmm. Well," he replied. "As you have given me the gift of your name, I give you the gift of mine and my dragon's. My dragon is Clarion, and I am Drannar. However, you may call me Dran. Everyone else does."

"Your servant, Dragonguard."

"My servant? Never, girl. The Dragonguard treat everyone equally, man and woman alike!"

Aya was confused and said so.

"I know that here in Danayalo, males rule the roost and females are second-class citizens at best, but among the Dragonguard, across the world, such absurd notions are ignored," Drannar explained.

"Things are different elsewhere?"

"Indeed, Danayalo is the only country I know of where such a social structure exists. You are the first female I have ever seen out walking on her own in Danayalo."

"I'm on my own, Drannar," she told him.

"Dran, girl, Dran," the Dragonguard insisted, and then changed the subject. "So you're not afraid of heights. Why is that? Most groundlings I have met are scared of anything higher than a rooftop, in my experience." There was a tone when he said *groundlings* that did not sound at all favorable.

"I've been climbing the very tall trees in the forest near our farm since I was a little girl. I loved looking down at everything below me when I did," she told Dran. "It's one of the few things I miss from where I used to live."

"What about your family?"

There it was: the question Aya had dreaded for so many months now. She supposed it would have come up, eventually, whoever she might have met. What would the Dragonguard do now? Would he take her back to the nightmare of her childhood?

"My mother is dead at the hand of my father, and my brother is little better than my father. I have nothing left there," she replied flatly. "I never want to go back. I'll be a midden-sweeper before I am Andagebi's daughter again."

Aya went silent and began to stroke the warm, smooth neck upon which she sat, willing herself not to cry at the sharp memory of her mother's terrible passing. She had supposed a dragon would be scaly, as other reptiles were, but Clarion's hide looked as though it was covered in tiny smooth pebbles.

"A pleasure to meet you, Clarion," she breathed. The dragon murmured a response. The Dragonguard who sat at her back chuckled.

"Of course, do that for the dragon, but not to me!"

Aya thought she had made some misstep, but then looked at the rider's face and saw that he was grinning down at her.

"No offense taken, Aya. I know that Clarion appreciates your recognition and manners." Once again, the dragon snorted. "Too often, people run away and hide when they see us coming."

"I've never run away when I've seen the Dragonguard in the sky," Aya proclaimed stoutly. "It has always made me feel safe to see them – you – up there, watching over us all. I always wanted the chance to meet a dragon, and now it has happened."

"Then you are the rare exception, gir – Aya," he replied. She noticed his abrupt substitution but affected not to have noticed.

"I've never ridden a dragon before," she said. "I never realized what it would be like!"

"Clarion and I have been together for the past thirty-two years, Aya. I think I have forgotten what it is like to walk long distances anymore. I have a difficult enough time making it from my bed to my front door!"

The dragon made a sound something like laughter, and Aya wondered why the dragon reacted that way. Perhaps it was some private joke between them both. She felt she should not have been surprised that dragons had a sense of humor. Surely, something so magnificent could not be merely a dumb beast, like a giant, flying cow

"Thirty-two years? How long does a dragon live," she gasped, and then wished she had not said such a thoughtless thing. How would she step back from that?

"A dragon and his rider live as long as the other does," Drannar told her.

"How old are you," she ventured carefully.

"Fifty-three," he replied with an amused smile.

"You don't look anywhere near that age!"

"A benefit of my relationship with Clarion, perhaps," he replied mysteriously and left it at that.

They had flown over a few villages before Aya realized that they were landing at none of them, and became concerned and finally said something about it.

"I'm taking you back to where I live," he told her, and Aya had to stop herself from wiggling free of him, knowing it would end very badly for her if she were successful.

"I don't want to go with you! I've already escaped a bad marriage!" she blurted. "I'm too young to be a wife!"

"Marriage? Whyever would you think that I wanted to bed you, much less marry you, girl?" he demanded. "I told you that women don't have to do what they are told in most of the world."

"Then why would you take me there?"

"Has it occurred to you that it might not be a good idea for a Dragonguard to visit a village?"

"Why could it be a bad idea? The Dragonguard watch over all of us!"

"There are very good reasons why it's not a good idea," he told her obliquely, chewing on a thick piece of dried meat that he had pulled from a pouch at his waist. He offered a piece to Aya, which she took gratefully. It had been a very long time since she had last eaten anything but a few early berries. "Beyond the unreasoning fear, there can be other problems."

"What problems," she pressed him when she had chewed up and swallowed her first bite. Drannar seemed to ignore her question. "Do dragons eat people?"

"We should arrive in a bit," he told her, not responding to her question. "Try to get some sleep until we do. I'll make sure you don't fall off."

From that point, they flew in silence, except for the occasional curious bird who would fly alongside them, chirping or crying out a challenge to the dragon, who ignored them all. It was clear that the beast held himself far above such minuscule denizens of the sky. He was a lord of all he surveyed and knew it.

Her jealousy rose again, and she fought to dampen it. She truly had no wish to offend, especially when she was far above the ground, with nothing between her and it but the dragon she rode. She felt a tremor go through the dragon's body and wondered how much of her thoughts or emotions it could sense.

10

The Dragonfort was on the side of a dormant volcano, its sides riddled with caves large and small. Clarion landed in a plaza of sorts, and his rider helped her down before dismounting as well. While humans seemed to be everywhere, she saw surprisingly few dragons in the area and wondered where they were.

What stunned Aya was the fact that she saw both men and women riding and walking with dragons, despite everything her father had told her. If he had been wrong about that, what else might he have been wrong about? Had he lied to her, or merely assumed how things were concerning the Dragonguard.

"Women can be Dragonguard, too?" she asked Dran breathlessly. "My father told me that only men could be Dragonguard."

"Well, then, he was wrong, wasn't he? Anyway, girl, if you are hungry, you can find the kitchens over there," he told her, pointing at a doorway festooned with bright bunting, before wandering off in another direction. "Just about anything you might like to eat will probably be available. Our cooks are quite gifted."

Aya ran up behind him.

"What am I supposed to do? I can't stay here!" she demanded of him.

"Let's wait until tomorrow morning, and we'll speak then," was his reply. "For now, eat. I am certain I heard your empty belly complain more than once, as we flew. Do as it demands and fill it!"

Realizing that Drannar was right, Aya went to the kitchen, as she had been bid, and saw foods there that she had only heard of, but never actually seen, much less eaten. Her stomach growled at her hungrily, as she breathed in the rich scent of the food around her. A sizeable roast turned on a spit up against the wall, and the scent of it near drove her mad. She was about to ask someone what she should do when a dark-haired young man approached her, a broad, welcoming smile on his face.

"What can I eat, please?" she asked him. "I don't want to take the wrong thing."

"If you would like something to eat, please help yourself to anything here," he told her. "Eat until you are satisfied."

"Anything? That can't be right," she objected. Aya had long ago learned that some treats were much too fine for a poor girl like her.

"Yes, anything. If it is out in the open, it's fair game for you."

Easily a dozen long tables had been set up in the cavern, with perhaps thirty or more people of both sexes sitting down at them. There did not appear to be any differentiation of social station, either. Well-dressed men and women sat and chatted elbow to elbow with men and women wearing what appeared to be threadbare clothing, and each seemed easy and happy in the others' company. Some rose to get their food and drink, while those who appeared to be kitchen staff served others, but as with the mix of status, there appeared to be the same kind of social blindness where serving was concerned. She stared as a man in a finely embroidered tunic brought a platter of sweets to a homely young woman who wore little more than rags.

Following directions she, Aya helped herself to a platter of well-marbled, bloody-rare beef, piled some green vegetables and several firm, bright red tomatoes alongside it, and went to sit in an available seat. A young woman came to her table and left a pitcher of something sweet smelling for her, along with an earthenware mug. Pouring some for herself and taking an experimental sip, she found it delicious, and happily drank it along with the beef and vegetables.

Aya had not realized how hungry she was before she had seen the bounty available in the kitchen cavern. Of course, having been on a very restricted diet for so long likely made her hunger greater than it might have been, as well.

She surprised herself by getting another large helping of beef and vegetables and finally finished it all off with a piece of hot fruit pie, topped with a thick slab of tasty yellow cheese. By the time she took the last bite, she was exhausted and almost fell asleep in her chair, belly distended with more food than she had had in one sitting over the past several months.

The next thing Aya knew, she was being carried out of the kitchen to some other location, but she was so tired, she was unable to speak to find out what was going on.

Wherever it was that they took her, there was a soft bed, with soft, comfortable blankets piled atop her. It was very quiet, and whoever had carried her there had a whispered conversation with someone else before they left.

As she slept, Aya had wild dreams. Swirls of rainbow color filled her mind. She felt as though she were thrashing around, but could not wake up, as much as she tried.

She felt as though she had eaten too much and that the food she had eaten was swelling in her belly and chest. It seemed to want to get *out* and get out *now*!

Real physical agony ripped through her body, coming in overwhelming waves. Aya tried to cry out in her sleep, but it was as though she was unable to open her mouth. Wave upon wave of pain shook her, and nothing she could do in her sleep was able to make it stop.

Eventually, the bloating agony seemed to go away, and truly exhausted in both mind and body, she settled into a deep, dreamless sleep, resting peacefully.

11

When she awoke, she could hear conversation coming from nearby, and she opened her eyes to see a small group of people standing in the doorway. She became aware of an odd sound nearby and looked up to see a blue dragon's massive head just above her own. It stared down at her with enormous, warm brown eyes that contained flashes of copper and gold. Knowing she should not be afraid of it, she reached up a hand and touched the tip of its jaw.

She gasped as she felt the whisper of the same touch on her jaw.

"What's going on?" she managed. "This doesn't make any sense!"

On the periphery of her vision, she saw someone step forward. When she turned her head to see better, Dran came into focus.

"This dragon is part of you, Aya. She was always in there, waiting to come out," he explained gently. "You told me that you always felt a special connection with dragons. This is the reason why you felt that way."

"That doesn't make any sense. How could I have a giant dragon inside of me?"

"Not everyone has it, Aya," Dran replied. "Clarion saw her within you the moment he and you touched one another. Once that contact was made, and he discovered her, we had to bring you here. Nothing would have stopped her emergence at that point. You would have been in mortal danger if someone had discovered you while you *Dreamed.*

You would have been vulnerable to capture, and that must never happen."

Aya heard a special stress on the word 'dreamed.'

"*Dreamed?*"

"That is how we describe a new dragon's emergence. I can think of no other way to express it," Dran finished, throwing up his hands. "I imagine that your dreams were odd as it all happened. Flashes of color, odd sounds, and sensations?"

Aya nodded, at a loss for words. It was all too much to comprehend.

"That is the *Dreaming* that happens as your dragon emerges. You have been unconscious for the better part of a week as she did. It does not happen quickly."

"But things must be born," she protested weakly. "I don't understand this at all!"

"Give yourself and your dragon time," Dran advised. "While you do, think of what your dragon's name might be. Your connection will grow even stronger, once she has a name."

"How am I supposed to know what her name it," Aya demanded.

"It will come to you. Don't worry about that. You just need to open your mind to knowing it," Dran assured her, then he left the room, shooing out the others before him. "Now, *eat*. You need the energy."

Only then did Aya become aware of the platter stacked with thick slices of bloody rare meat that sat on her bedside table, alongside a tall mug of something that steamed invitingly. Without thinking, she began shoving slices of the rich meat into her mouth, chewing perfunctorily before washing them down with what proved to be hot tea.

"And get some sleep. *Real* sleep!" She heard Drannar laugh. "You can finish your food later on if you are too tired to finish it now."

Soon, Aya was left alone with the great dragon, who looked down at her and then reached out a gigantic paw. Putting out her hand, she placed it in the center of the dragon's palm. The combined touch was disconcerting but felt "right" to her.

"So you're a part of me, are you?"

The dragon, of course, did not say anything, but instead made a noise that sounded sort of like agreement to Aya. She felt the dragon's assent in her head, much like when she had a conversation with herself in her head, but it was not actual words.

"How could you have been inside of me," she asked, and then chuckled to herself in dismay. "I shouldn't be asking you questions you can't answer, should I?"

The dragon shifted and laid down on her belly, stretching and curving her neck around so she could rest the tip of her nose on Aya's chest while continuing to stare into her eyes. Aya was surprised to find that the dragon's head had no weight at all for her, although it did have substance enough to touch it with her hand, and she was unable to move beneath it.

"So you want me to sleep as well, do you?"

The dragon blinked at her, the first time she had done so since they "met." Aya took that for assent. A wave of exhaustion overtook her, and she realized that the dragon had been acting to keep her awake, but was now letting that tiredness back in. Her eyelids became heavy, and then closed, and Aya slept.

Some time later, Aya had no idea how long that might have been, she awoke. The dragon's head rested at her side, and she saw that the creature's eyes were open and looking at her. She realized she was once again ravenous and realized the dragon might be feeling the same way.

"Are you hungry?"

A feeling of negation came to her. That seemed odd.

"How could you not be hungry? I ate, but you didn't." Aya reached for the half-empty platter on her side table and tried giving it to the dragon, who turned her head away.

"That's because she's part of you, and you eat for the both of you," Dran said as he walked into the room, not bothering to knock to announce himself. The dragon turned her head toward the approaching Dragonguard and gave him an unfriendly look.

"Oh, bother that, youngling," he scolded the creature as he approached Aya's pallet. "I'm old enough to be her grandfather! I'm not going to hurt her."

The dragon grumbled at him, clearly unhappy with the affable Dragonguard, but did not offer to hurt him.

"You need to get to the kitchens and eat something fresh, young Aya," he told the girl. "Don't let yourself go too long without eating."

"Why is that?" she asked, putting the piece of cold meat back on the platter with its fellows, but Dran seemed to ignore her question.

"Up, up, up with you!" he prodded at her, and, suiting actions to words, pulled the blankets off her and made as though to pick her up.

The dragon roared with rage at his temerity, and appearing to recollect himself, Dran stepped back from the bed, hands raised in a gesture of peace and self-protection.

"I'm only trying to get her out into the sun, dragon," he protested. "I told you I would never hurt her, as though you would ever allow that to happen, anyway!"

Not wanting to see anyone become hurt, Aya rose from her bed and wrapped the shawl she had found folded on the table next to her around her shoulders. The dragon kept a protective eye on Aya, still glaring at Dran for the liberties he had taken with her human half.

"Okay, I'll go to the kitchens, but how is the dragon supposed to get out of the room? The door's much too small for her," Aya stepped out the door, into the daylight, and turned to watch what the dragon would do.

To her surprise, the dragon simply followed her to the door, and then went *through* the wall itself, as though it was not even there. Aya gasped and wavered in her tracks as she felt faint.

"Your dragon isn't a physical being, Aya," she dimly heard Dran telling her. "It is a part of your life energy. It only has as much substance as is necessary. If you need to fly together, she will have enough for you to sit on her back, but most times, it will be as you just saw."

"I – "

"Just go to the kitchens and eat as much as you need. Think of it as eating for the both of you. If you don't eat, your dragon will have trouble staying solid when you need her to be, and that could be dangerous for you both."

Aya obediently wandered back to the kitchen cavern and availed herself of a hearty meat-based stew that warmed her all over and could have fit the description of food that would "stick to your ribs." The young man he had met on her first day at the Dragonfort gave her another broad smile and came over with a cup of something that steamed merrily.

"This should help you to wake up a bit more," he told her. "Drink it down, and I'll refill it when I see you need more."

She took the cup and sniffed at its contents. Aya had never seen or smelled anything like it before. It was a dark brown color, and had a kind of minty aroma, but was otherwise unfamiliar to her.

"What is this," she asked the young man, who had not yet wandered off.

"It's tea," he said. "Have you never had tea before?"

"No, I haven't. We usually drank ale or cow's milk with our meals," Aya replied. "We did not have the money for such things as *tea*."

"Well, it's a staple item here, and you can find some at almost any hour of the day or night, should you desire it."

"Why would I desire it?"

"It will help to wake you and then keep you awake. You will find that is sometimes necessary, in your new life."

"New life?"

"As a Dragonguard, of course!" the young man laughed. "My name, by the way, is Jarrod,"

"A pleasure to meet you, Jarrod," she responded. "My name is Aya."

"Dran told us," Jarrod said. "I'm glad you've joined us."

"Are you a Dragonguard?"

"Of course I am. Everyone here is a Dragonguard."

"Where's your dragon, then?"

"Oh, Ebony is out flying around, having fun," Jarrod said. "He doesn't like being holed up in the Dragonfort all the time."

"Your dragon can do that? Fly without you?"

"Of course he can. Yours will be able to do the same thing, in time. It has to do with the strength of your bond. The stronger it is, the stronger your dragon will be. So, eat up and then get more rest. The *Dreaming* takes a lot out of you," and with that, Jarrod disappeared into the back of the kitchen cavern.

Aya went back for seconds, and then thirds, before her appetite was sated. Jarrod ended up bringing a small pot of the tea to her since she drank it down almost faster than he could come back to refill it. She knew it would be something she would have as often as she could manage.

12

Two weeks later, and Aya still had not come up with a name for her dragon. It was not that she had not thought about it, it was just that nothing seemed appropriate as a name for the great beast.

Dran teased her about it relentlessly, offering several inappropriate suggestions when Aya once again admitted her ignorance. He would laugh when some of them got a rise out of her. That often led to a half-hearted chase through the buildings and cavern facilities.

Despite their vast difference in age, he reminded her of how she had always thought a brother and sister relationship should be, and she loved him for it.

For now, Aya had three substantial meals a day, but none of the extra protein calories went to her hips. As she understood it, those extra calories went to keeping her dragon solid. If she went too long, she would still be able to *see* her dragon but would be unable actually to touch her, much less fly her.

One day, when she experimented, she discovered that at least two meals a day were required to keep the dragon corporeal. Aya had been very uncomfortable, and unusually ravenous, and so she decided she would never experiment in that away again.

Aya had not yet started riding patrols. It was explained to her that a new dragon and rider pair spent their first few months getting to know one another. Until she at least knew her dragon's name, she would not be put on patrol. There was, she was assured more than once, no shame in this. With some pairings, it took time.

Aya took the opportunity to decorate the room designated as her quarters. She had been given an amazingly soft, freshly sewn bed, and a down comforter. It was very different from the musty, straw-stuffed pallet she had grown up using in the corner of the main room of the cottage. No longer was she poked by itchy straw as she slept. Instead, she slept happily and comfortably.

It was strange, there was no doubt about it, to have something outside of you that was also a part of you. Initially, Aya was startled and confused by the sensations coming from things that she, herself, did not touch.

It seemed that one of the lessons upon which the most care was taken, was in creating a mental wall to keep one from going mad from these disembodied sensations. On the other hand, Aya loved it when her dragon would fly, riderless, up high, and looked down at the world below her. She learned to close her eyes and open her mind to experiencing those sights from the eyes of her dragonself.

Drannar had explained to her that there were very few individuals who possess the ability to *Dream* a dragon. Most of those special people who were 'found' were from specific bloodlines. It was quite unusual to find one from what appeared to be a completely unconnected source.

Aya wondered if perhaps there might have been someone in her mother's family tree that might have given this gift to her. She knew it would help to explain why she had always felt the way she had at the mere sight of a dragon. The dragon that waited inside of her would stir, trying to find a way to rise and fly with her mates.

No one knew how the human/dragon pairings had begun because in this time, a gifted human needed to be physically touched by a dragon for the *Dreaming* to begin. The Dragonguard kept the entire process a close secret, as they did not want such information to get out to the wrong sort of people. Aya imagined wholesale breeding of potentially gifted children to build airborne armies and then shuddered at that thought.

The Dragonguard communities kept mostly to themselves and found their relationships and mates from among their kind. They found it to be the best way to both have a better opportunity for increasing their numbers and for keeping their origins a secret.

Aya had discovered that the more active she and her dragon were, the hungrier she would be, and the more food she would consume. It was worth noting that none of the Dragonguard was so much as overweight. She was, in truth, eating for two.

Because of their greatly increased mobility, the Dragonguard had taken it upon themselves to be the guardians of their world. They quickly squashed disputes between countries that escalated into anything resembling violence. They did not rule, but they maintained a peaceful order to the world.

There were several dozen Dragonguard enclaves throughout the world. Most were in places that were difficult, if not impossible, to reach by those who used more traditional methods of travel.

On occasion, an outsider might try to infiltrate an enclave, but they were usually quickly discovered and removed. If gentle dissuasion was not successful, individuals who were more tenacious were unofficially adopted and moved to an enclave far from their point of origin. While they might never experience a *Dreaming*, they were given a place in the community and put to work.

There was one such individual in this enclave, who was called Sundance. A mere boy when he had painstakingly climbed his way into the heights that contained the enclave, black-haired Lauro did not take "no" for an answer when he had made his petition to be a Dragonguard. A decision had been made to transport the child half a world away from his birth village, and he would now live out the remainder of his life forever separated from his family and childhood friends.

Lauro's family members had not been left ignorant of the child's fate but had been told that he would become a part of the greater Dragonguard community. The Dragonguard were not heartless, after all.

Six years had passed since that time, and Lauro was content simply to live among the dragons and their people. He was a year older than Aya, and while not notably handsome, he was not unattractive, either. He earned his keep by maintaining the quarters of several of the Dragonguard, making sure they remained neat and tidy.

Although he already had a significant number of apartments assigned to his care, Lauro had volunteered to add Aya's apartment to his roster. She suspected the young man was interested in her as more than a friend, but she kept him at an emotional distance. Even though her circumstances had changed for the better, she still had no interest in that kind of a relationship with anyone.

Aya found it pleasant, after a long day, to come home and find her quarters clean, dusted, and smelling faintly of the fresh flowers that Lauro would leave in the vase on her dresser. At first, it seemed strange to her that someone else would be taking care of her basic needs, but she came to enjoy having had that responsibility lifted from her shoulders. Aya would have been happy never to have to clean again, but that would have been silly and selfish, which she was not.

The tome from the abandoned village had a place of honor as the only resident of a shelf carved out of the stone wall of her chambers. Aya would take it down late at night, and look at it by the light of the single tallow candle that cut through the chamber's nighttime darkness. She knew that some of the people of Sundance knew how to read, but had not yet summoned the courage to find out who and ask them to teach her that mystic art.

The curious walking stick, which was unneeded at this point, rested in a well-lit corner of her quarters. At her request, Lauro kept it dusted, and had polished it to a brilliant shine.

As did all the Dragonguard, Aya would take her turn in the kitchens, and added some of her favorite recipes to those that were already known. Kitchen duties ranged everywhere from meal preparation to cooking to the washing of soiled utensils and dishes.

Yes. Real dishes. No worn, cracked wooden trencher platters and bowls that were barely holding on. The dishes' construction ranged from wood to stone and even ceramic. Some of the ceramic dishes seemed too fine to Aya to be used as everyday items, but she soon learned that there were even finer ceramic dishes that had been tucked away for special functions. These were crafted of such fine china that one could see the brightness glow from behind when they were held up to a light source. They were glorious, as far as Aya was concerned.

Every day brought something new for Aya, and she reveled in the discoveries she made. Her former life had been predictable and boring, and now that was no longer the case. She felt free, emotionally and physically, and it was almost more than she could bear, but she loved it, just the same.

13

"Aya, where did you get that?" Dran asked her one day during breakfast, pointing at the walking stick, which she had brought out for an anticipated afternoon walk in the heavily treed mountains that lay a league or so to the north. His question brought her up short, as Dran normally called her "youngster," or "girl," rather than by her given name. For the man to use her given name was unusual.

"This? I found it in the basement of the town hall in that abandoned village where I stayed after I ran away from home, Dran," she replied, after hastily swallowing her mouthful of the spicy cheese and tomato omelet she had chosen for breakfast. She started to pass it over to him. "It looks odd, doesn't it? Do you know what it's made of because I have no clue."

The Dragonguard leaned in close for a look but declined to touch the walking stick. From his expression, she could tell that he knew what it was, so why he had asked her about it was confusing. Why ask about something about which you already knew, but she played along.

"You found this? Truly? It was not *given* to you?"

"Whoever owned it either left it behind or was one of the skeletons down in that basement, Dran. It was clear he or she did not need it anymore."

The Dragonguard, a perplexed expression on his face, peered at the staff, still not touching it.

"You can hold it if you like, Dran. It's not as though it would bite you!" Aya laughed.

The Dragonguard made a face and stepped back, raising both hands in front of his face as though warding off an attack.

"Not bite me? You have no idea. Aya, girl, that thing is dangerous!"

"Dangerous? It's just a pretty walking stick!"

"No, girl, it's far more than that. It is made from *vaasahorn*," he replied. "What you have is something quite rare."

"What is a vasha?" she asked, mispronouncing the unfamiliar name.

"A *vaasa* is a tall, slender creature that bears a single horn at the top of its head, between its ears. The horn grows for three or more years before it is finally shed, and another begins to grow in its place."

"So, like a deer grows antlers, then, not like a billy goat's horn," she responded. When she was younger, she would often be sent to gather shed deer antlers for her father's occasional knife repair tasks.

"Not really, no," he said. "That horn has strange properties. It cannot be stolen successfully. Ever. Thieves tend to come to very bad ends when they attempt it."

Aya stared at the stick in her hand, disbelief showing on her face. She shivered as a thrill of fear shot through her.

"It is clear that you did not steal it, or you would not have survived its touch," Dran told her. Aya suddenly remembered the skeletons she had found in the basement, and wondered what, exactly, had happened to cause their deaths. A wave of nausea rippled through her, and she gagged.

"You are fine, Aya. If there had been anything amiss, I doubt you would have made it more than five steps before you joined the other residents of that basement," he said reassuringly. "Keep an eye on that thing, and whatever you do, if you need someone to touch it, give them permission, first."

"Dran, you need to tell me—" she interjected.

"No, Aya. That thing scares me to my bones. I don't want to be anywhere near it," he said. "Not for now, anyway. Have a good day and spend some time thinking of a name for that dragon of yours. You can't just call her 'Dragon' forever, you know."

With that, the Dragonguard rose and went off to start his daily patrol, leaving Aya staring at the thing she had until just now considered to be no more than a very ornate walking staff.

14

Going outside one morning after breaking her fast, she found her dragon (*her dragon!*) waiting for her. Although she knew the creature was also her, it had its own sense of awareness and desires.

"Was there something you wanted?" she asked the creature, who had something on her mind. "What is it?"

Not even taking a moment to glance at her, the dragon hunched down, and Aya instantly understood that she was to climb onto her dragon's shoulders. Obliging the wordless request, she then suddenly found herself in the air, the dragon's enormous wings beating at the air lazily. It was then that Aya realized the dragons did not *have* to beat their wings to stay aloft. It was something else entirely that kept them in the air.

"Where are we going?"

The dragon, of course, said nothing, but simply began flying with a purpose. Helpless against her dragon's determination, Aya watched as the landscape changed below them.

It was not long before the landscape began to look slightly more familiar, and Aya realized their destination, beginning to worry.

"No! Dragon! Not that!"

The dragon continued to ignore her entreaties and kept flying. It was even more evident that even though the creature was a part of her, the dragon had a mind of her own.

Knowing there was nothing she could do, Aya sat back and watched the ground pass below the dragon's massive wings as she flew. As they flew over the abandoned village that had Aya's home for almost half a year, she saw that there was smoke coming from the chimney of the cottage she had lived in. For some reason, it made her feel good to know that someone else was living there now. There was even a small garden next to the front door.

This appeared to be someone who was not in hiding, unlike Aya, who had been forced to conceal her presence in the village to stay safe. She silently wished whoever it was well, as the stone walls disappeared from her field of view.

The flight gave Aya a much better idea of how far she had traveled, between her new home and her old one. The part she had walked was daunting, and knowing that what had taken her weeks to traverse was crossed in a matter of mere hours.

Perhaps four hours later, Aya saw the even more familiar landmarks of her old home and saw that her father and probably her brother had rebuilt the cottage. The dragon landed a short distance from the cottage and then abruptly disappeared, as though she had never existed. Still, Aya could feel that she was with her, even though she could not see her.

The dog lay near the front door, opening her eyes, and thumping her tail weakly against the ground. The heavily graying animal, now much skinnier than Aya remembered, did not make a sound.

Feigning a bravery she did not feel, she approached the new stone cottage, and the wooden door opened, to reveal her father. The expression on his face changed from dull curiosity to rage, as he realized who stood there.

"Aya! You ungrateful little slut, when I get through with you – "
He never finished his sentence.

Aya's dragon appeared out of nowhere, in the much more massive form she would sometimes take, her eyes flashing like fire, and her father stopped short, throwing his arms in front of his face in a protective gesture, a short scream escaping his lips.

"Dragonguard! Where is the Dragonguard?" he demanded in terror. He looked around wildly. "Why are they here?"

"You're looking at her, Andagebi," she replied, disdaining to give him his parental honorific. "She is mine. I only came to tell you goodbye, and to let you know you will never see me again."

"You? A Dragonguard? You are a girl. That's not possible!" he scoffed. "You're neither highborn nor male. Where is the *real* Dragonguard, *girl*?"

He made her gender sound like an insult.

"You need to pay more attention to the riders, then, father," she snorted. "Both men and women can be Dragonguard. You don't know as much as you pretend."

Anger clouded his face, and Andagebi forgot himself and took another a step toward his daughter, fist raised to strike. The dragon swung her massive head down between them, interposing herself between father and daughter. Andagebi stepped back again.

Enjoying the look of fear on his face, Aya reached up a hand and scratched the dragon's jawline, a smug expression on her face as she did so. The look on her father's face was priceless as the dragon hummed a happy sound and closed her eyes until they were half-lidded.

Andagebi, not the brightest star in the sky, stepped forward again, and Aya straightened. He began to reach out a hand to touch the dragon, but Aya intercepted his filthy hand.

"Do *not* touch my dragon, Andagebi!" she spat.

Feeling Aya's anger at her father, the dragon snapped at the man. She was sure the inside of her dragon's mouth was terrifying to behold. While the creature might not eat, she could and did bite when necessary.

"I've not forgotten what you did to Mother," she told him, her rage loosening her tongue. "She told me about my sisters, too. The ones you murdered. I hope Gebi's new wife knows that her daughters are in danger from their grandfather."

"Daughters are useless. I did not want more daughters," he replied dismissively, anger still burning in his eyes. "You were burden enough."

"You are a murderer, like that baker you planned to sell me to as a wife."

"Your mother was telling you tales," he protested. "He is a fine man. You would have had a fine house in town."

"Fine house or not, I was not going to marry some old man. You did not care that his last wife died suspiciously. What kind of marriage was Gebi sold into? Has his new wife started popping out new farmhands for you?"

"Loris and Gebi did not marry," her father said in disgust. "The contract was canceled because of the fire. The dowry was lost."

The dowry was lost. Was that all that was important to Aya's father? She knew it was nonsense even to suggest otherwise.

It was clear that Andagebi had cared more for his gain than anyone's happiness. His selfish attitude only made Aya angrier.

She was so angry that she forgot that her dragon would be a mirror of that growing anger.

"Good. You and Gebi can live with yourselves."

"Gebiarno did not return after he went to find *you*," Andagebi said quietly, although his eyes had not lost their anger. "I do not know where he went."

A growl murmured through the air.

"Good," she replied with a smile, much cockier, as her dragon was there to protect her from the kind of violence that had led to Zoraya's death. She was pleased to know that her brother had taken his leave of his father and the family farm as soon as he was able. "The farther away from you, the better."

Andagebi began to sputter with apoplectic rage and shook his dirty fist in her face. Aya stood her ground, not giving even an inch.

The murmuring growl changed to something more intense.

Aya did not even flinch at her father's proximity.

Enraged by Aya's stance, words, and evident pleasure, Andagebi soon forgot himself and moved toward his daughter. His work-gnarled fingers reached out to grab her shoulders –

The growl became a roar of intractable rage.

Andagebi screamed as the dragon knocked Aya aside and then let loose with a blast of blue flame that wreathed up around the screaming man. Much hotter than natural fire, the flames instantly blackened Andagebi's flesh, and moved inward to his bones.

Andagebi's scream of agony climbed the register to become a high, porcine squeal, and then abruptly ceased as the flames took his life. Was it too soon, or not quickly enough? Aya had no answer to that thought.

She stood up and watched as the dancing blue flames burned her sire to ashes, unsympathetic and unmoved by his demise. As his corpse burned away to nothing, the day seemed to brighten, and she felt a great weight lift from her shoulders.

The air stank of grilling sausages and Aya wondered in passing if she would ever be able to enjoy them again. She filed that thought away for later experimentation.

The lives Andagebi had damaged, but not destroyed during his long reign of terror would be better with his presence removed from the world. His carcass burned a long time, and Aya stood there, watching as her father became nothing but an unidentifiable mound of embers on the ground.

"You should have paid attention when she warned you off the first time," she said to what remained, in a scolding tone. "She'd never have let you lay a finger on me. Now, you'll never terrorize anyone again."

She looked up at the dragon and reached out a hand to scratch a chin the size of her head. Someone who did not know where dragons came from would have marveled at her sheer bravery in doing so.

The dragon stared down at her, confusion in her enormous, beautiful eyes, a confusion that mirrored what Aya felt at that moment. Should she climb on board and fly away to parts unknown, or should she own what she had done and tell Dran, allowing the die to fall where it would?

Of course, she would go back, tell Dran what had happened, and leave herself to the justice of the Council. One did not run away from things that were truly important. A Dragonguard took responsibility.

Aya wondered how the dragon had acted on her own if she was simply a reflection of her human self. Somehow, she had responded on her own, without Aya anticipating what she would do and perhaps stepping in. She had watched and, perhaps, thought about what she saw, and then had acted when Aya was given a real threat of bodily harm.

"How did you do that, big girl?" she asked the dragon. The beast licked gently at her hand, a comforting gesture for them both. "You looked out for me when I needed you most."

It was as though she heard a *ping* in her head.

You looked out for me when I needed you most.

You looked out for me.

Like a watchman. A guardian. A sentinel.

"Sentinel," she said firmly. "Your name is Sentinel!"

The freshly named dragon chirped a happy response and went off to bother the hogs, who were terrified at the monster that loomed over their pen. They had no idea she was not a danger to them, and Aya had to admit to herself that it was amusing to watch the beasts scatter as Sentinel sniffed their backs.

Gebi had probably followed Aya's example, once the wolves had stopped chasing him. She had no real interest in finding him, as she was still angry that he had left their mother to be beaten to death, but she hoped he found some happiness, wherever he was now.

Aya was distressed to see that Sentinel seemed slightly translucent. That could only mean one thing, and lessons she had learned shortly after her *Dreaming* came back to her, reminding her that this was very important. The release of flame must have taken extra energy from the dragon that she might not otherwise have expended, and she could now see the results of that.

Aware that she was now very hungry, Aya went into the rebuilt cottage and saw a pot of cold porridge atop a rude wooden table. Andagebi had never been good at cooking, and the few times Zoraya had been too ill to cook, porridge was the order of the day.

Grabbing the wooden spoon from the pot, she began shoveling the otherwise unappetizing sludge and shoveled it down. Yes, it was as she remembered it. Mostly grain, with some meat cooked down to the point where it had fallen apart and was now unidentifiable to the naked eye.

While it tasted bland, salty, but not bad, Aya knew it would give her dragon the strength she now lacked, and would then be able to fly the two of them back to Sundance, where she would face what she had done to her father.

To be able to swallow it down, she focused on the fact that she was doing this for Sentinel. The dragon was the most important thing in the world to her, and she wanted her well away from the sadness and desolation that was the home of her youth.

After opening the barn door and blocking it with a suitable stone, Aya took the time to free the remaining livestock, this time for good, as the odds of a visitor coming to call were not much. The old sow was still there, along with her now half-grown offspring. The two wandered off toward the ripening crops, grunting with contentment.

The cow and her calf moved, as one, to the tall mounds of blue-green hay stacked on the shaded side of the barn. Not the most energetic of creatures at the best of times, and with easy food so close, the cow would eat the hay down to the last straw before moving on to the bounty of the fields. Her still-suckling calf would now have all of its mother's milk, instead of having to share it with humans.

When she went to check on the chickens, Aya found the coop long deserted by poultry, but now inhabited by a half dozen opportunistic wild pigeons and their noisy, messy hatchlings. All of Aya's careful cleaning was now undone, replaced with tall piles of gray and white pigeon guano.

At least she would no longer be expected to clean the rickety old coop, but she wondered what condemnation awaited her back home, once she told Dran and the rest of Sundance about what she had done, and if they would ever forgive her for doing it.

Climbing aboard Sentinel, she started her long flight home. Understanding that Aya did not want to rush back, the dragon took the flight at as slow a speed as was possible, considering her energy limitations.

14

"Dran... I have to talk to you about something, but in private," she said when she found the older Dragonguard alone. Sentinel was wherever dragons went when they were not with their human selves. "Please."

Aya did not want an extended audience for whatever Dran's reaction would be when he learned what she and Sentinel had done. How much would he hate her? How disappointed would he be?

He raised an eyebrow at her words, scrutinizing her face as if seeking answers in her expression.

"What is it, Aya," he finally asked her kindly, directing her to sit on the low rock wall behind him, and then sitting. He patted the open space next to him invitingly. "What could be so serious?"

"I killed my father!" she blurted, collapsing onto the sun-warmed wall and then bursting into tears. Instead of making an exclamation, Dran enfolded her with his good arm and pulled her in toward his chest, Aya's tears soaking into the soft fabric of his best tunic.

"I can't imagine you doing something like that. What happened?"

"He tried to grab me, and Sentinel set him on fire!"

"Sentinel? She has a name now?"

"Y-yes," she stammered. Aya expected to hear condemnation from him, but it did not come. Drannar seemed more interested in the fact that Aya's dragon was no longer nameless.

"I don't want to go to prison, but she – I – we – killed a man!"

"You said he tried to grab you? You didn't tell Sentinel to do it?"

"No, I didn't, but if Sentinel and I are the same, then I did it, didn't I? It's all my fault!" She could not catch her breath and began gasping for air.

"Calm down, Aya. Just calm down. Relax and try to breathe." He stroked her back soothingly. "Don't panic, Aya. Don't panic."

"What am I going to do?"

"He tried to grab you, and Sentinel acted to protect you. Did she warn him off, first?"

"Well, she *did* get in his way more than once and growled at him, but he wanted to hurt me," she allowed. "I did say some bad things to him, though."

"Only words? You never touched him?"

Aya shook her head, confused. It would never have occurred to her to attempt to slap her father.

"Then, whatever you may have said to him, that would never excuse his trying to hurt you."

"I'm afraid, Dran," she told him, staring up into his face. "I'm so scared. I have a good home now, and I do not want to lose it! I don't want to lose the friends and the life I've made here."

"I think you'll be okay, but we'll both speak to the Council in the morning, and then they will decide what's to be done. Tell them everything, and do not leave anything out. Always be honest with them, and they'll be honest with you, too."

15

Facing the entire Council had been one of the hardest things Aya had done in her entire life, but she knew that it had to be done. In the time since she had joined the Dragonguard, she had found them to be fair and reasonable in their decisions, in addition to being the administration of the minutiae of daily life in the Dragonguard, dealing out both justice and mercy as needed. A male and a female worked as co-leaders, with another six Councilmembers assisting, three females, and three males. It was the complete antithesis of how her father had always told his family the world worked.

They had first spoken with Drannar about what she had told him, then she had been called in, and the Council had spent the better part of three hours grilling her on what had happened between her and her father that ended in his horrific death.

Aya had lost track of how many times they asked her to repeat the events of that day; she just knew that by the time they had dismissed her to begin their deliberations, she had been exhausted down to her bones.

Gy'yara, the female Council leader, had been meticulous in her questioning of events. She wanted to know every little detail of the day and Aya's life before she left her family.

Tennon, the male Council leader, was a small, almost nondescript man, someone who would probably occasion little notice in the outside world, were his dragon nowhere in sight. He had been a kinder interrogator than Gy'yara had, but no less thorough.

The other Council members had asked fewer questions, but they all appeared to bear their complete attention on the matter at hand.

Before the meeting, Drannar had told Aya that the Journaler, as she was called, would write down everyone's words. Aya wondered how anyone could do something so thoroughly and be able to keep up with what was being said, but somehow, she did. The Journaler took copious notes during the entire process, entering the discussion into a leather-bound journal as they spoke. Once in a while, a Councilmember might ask the Journaler to repeat something that had already been said, and she would dutifully read it out to them.

Several hours later, Aya was dismissed, and she went to her quarters, wondering what punishment she would face for the crime she had committed. She was not hungry, and even Lauro could not tempt her with what he knew to be her favorite foods. Instead, she curled up on her bed, facing the wall and weeping. Only when Dran forced the issue did she finally leave her rooms, but then she went to the farthest corner of the hold and sat alone, except for the constant attendance of her dragon.

16

The Council signaled that its business was completed, but the assembly did not rise to leave. Something was up, but she had no idea what that might be. As she looked around to see was going on, she heard someone call her name, and looked back toward the dais. Dran had stood up, and was beckoning to her.

Knowing that she was going to get into trouble for Sentinel's killing of her father, but also knowing she had no alternative, Aya reluctantly went to join him. She wondered if she would be banished from the Dragonfort for what she had done, but decided that whatever her punishment, she would accept it. As long as she had her dragon with her, she could survive anything.

Of course, the time had come, and Aya's sentence was about to be pronounced. The respite she had enjoyed could not have lasted indefinitely. All good things..., and all that.

In the time since her interrogation by the Council, Aya had been living her life through rote action, not paying attention to the world around her, as she knew that the freedom she had come to love over the short time she had been a Dragonguard was about to be torn away.

The older Dragonguard put his hands on her shoulders and looked into her eyes, appearing to search for something. Aya steeled herself for the condemnation to come.

"The Council has discussed the unfortunate situation of what happened to your sire, Andagebi. He died a terrible death. That cannot be denied," Drannar declared.

Aya nodded, wordless.

The Councilmembers simply looked at her, their faces unreadable. She stood as still as she could, but it was difficult not to fidget under their steely regard.

"At the Council's behest, I investigated Andagebi and discovered that he had an unwholesome reputation. Many who knew him told me that he was an unusually cruel man. With the knowledge that he also murdered your defenseless infant sisters, it is clear that he would not hesitate to kill again. Those who would kill a child will have no trouble doing so again."

"But I — Sentinel — killed him! A man is dead because of me! He was not a good man, but that does not excuse what I did," Aya cried, stricken. "I need to be punished for what I did!"

"Aya, you have been punishing yourself for what happened ever since it happened. It is clear that you have great remorse for his death," said Gy'yara from the Council table. "Don't think we have not noticed your demeanor, child."

"You did not know it, but Andagebi was in the process of arranging another marriage for himself. A young woman who would be able to bear him more children. Imagine what he would have done with another daughter," Drannar told her. "No, Sentinel did the right thing in moving to protect you, but I would encourage you not to make a habit of taking justice into your hands in the future."

He squeezed her shoulders encouragingly but did not release his grip. Instead, he drew her in close to his chest and let her cry herself out as he held her. She held tight to the Dragonguard as though he might slip from her grasp and go away, never to be seen again.

Several minutes had passed before Drannar spoke again.

"And finally, Aya, it has occurred to the Council that you still have only half a name, and with your *Dreaming*, you are surely deserving of the second half of your name," Dran told her, with a reassuring smile.

"My family's tradition was that my future husband would give me my second name, Dran. I no longer have a family to arrange a marriage, so I will have to make do with my simple, childish Aya," she looked down to hide the sadness on her face as she spoke.

Dran chuckled, and Clarion nosed Aya from behind, startling the girl into raising her head, where she saw something dancing in the man's eyes.

"Aya, girl, you have a new family now, which is something you don't seem to understand," he explained. "A family who loves and cares about you, and who want you to be happy."

"A new family," she asked, confused by Drannar's words.

"Firstly, you will not marry unless you decide you wish to do so, and it will only be for love."

Aya stared at her friend, not comprehending what he was telling her.

Lauro emerged from the crowd that stood on the periphery of the cavern and crossed to where Drannar and Aya stood. He cradled a small wooden box in both hands, which he then gave to Drannar. The Dragonguard opened it, showing its contents to her.

Inside the box was a ring made of polished bronze, exquisitely worked into the shape of a dragon. Sliding it on each finger until she found one it would fit, she saw that it was sized to fit around her right index finger.

She held up her hand, showing the precious gift to all assembled.

"As of this day, you are Dran'aya," he said. "Does anyone here question or challenge my adoption of this young woman as my true daughter?"

The loud cheer that greeted his question coming from all those assembled was all the answer Dran'aya needed to hear, and she jumped into the arms of her adopted father, both Sentinel and Clarion roaring their enthusiastic approval.

Did you like what you read, because there *will* be more stories about Aya, Sentinel, and the Dragonguard! Keep your eyes open for more!

Don't miss out!

Visit the website below and you can sign up to receive emails whenever Anna Rose publishes a new book. There's no charge and no obligation.

https://books2read.com/r/B-A-MFMF-YPTQ

BOOKS 2 READ

Connecting independent readers to independent writers.

About the Author

Anna Rose is the author of the Tales of the Dragonguard (about dragons, of course!) and The Sumaire Web series of vampire novels.

She is currently working on KAL'S HEART, the third story in the Tales of the Dragonguard, that began with AYA'S DRAGON, and continues with SARA'S FIRE. which is now available in both e-book and softcover at Amazon, and in ebook format at iTunes, Barnes & Noble, and other fine merchants.

KAL'S HEART continues the story of the high-flying Dragonguard. Kal, the Aerie-born son of Dragonguard parents, is faced with a mystery that affects not only the whole of the Dragonguard, but his family as well. Together, he and his unusual dragon, Spirit, must use their unique abilities to find out who is causing trouble for the Dragonguard and to his family.

Her newest venture with her stories and novels is turning them into audiobooks for those folks who prefer listening to books, rather than reading them, for whatever reason.

Amongst her other writing, Anna writes vampires who like what they are and aren't looking for a rescue. Her vampires bite, drink and kill. No bottled or bagged blood for these vampires!

The first novel in the series, SIOFRA, was released in late January of 2012. The first novel was followed by FIACH FOLA and then DROCH FOLA. There is also a short story called FEASTA FOLA. Anna is also working on the fourth novel in the Sumaire Web series, COSAN FOLA, which she hopes to have completed by the end of 2018.

She lives in usually sunny Southern California.

Read more at www.sumaire.com.

www.ingramcontent.com/pod-product-compliance
Lightning Source LLC
Chambersburg PA
CBHW020630130626
46552CB00003B/1161